Lexie WANTS TO GET THE GUY:

All January, all Lexie had thought about was Dylan Easterby. Of course, she'd always had a tiny crush on him—what girl didn't get a thrill from Dylan? You'd have to be dead. Which, technically speaking, Lexie kind of was.

Maddy WANTS TO KNOW HER NEIGHBORS:

"I'm your neighbor," said Maddy, "and since the door was open, I came over to introduce myself."

"Our door is never open," said the woman at the same time the man said, "We are Nigel and Nicola von Krik. How exciting for us to meet a fresh new neighbor."

"And you are a . . . human being?" asked Nicola.

"Of course. One hundred percent." Untrue, but Maddy was surprised. Her human beingness had never been questioned before. Was she imagining things, or had Nigel just licked his lips?

Hudson WANTS TO SEE THE WORLD... AND MAKE IT A BETTER PLACE:

"Fly around the park, but that's it, Sport," his mother always reminded him.

"And if your grades drop, that's it for flight privileges," added his father.

His parents knew Hudson had the most bat in him. He was the only Livingstone who needed to sleep upside down, who communicated with other species, and who could shape-shift for a single, glorious predawn hour into the Old World creature he'd once been.

VAMPIRE
ISLAND

ADELE GRIFFIN

SCHOLASTIC INC.
New York Toronto London Auckland
Sydney Mexico City New Delhi Hong Kong

ISBN: 978-0-545-22392-8

12 11 10 9 8 7 6 5 4 3   10 11 12 13 14/0

Printed in the U.S.A.   40

First Scholastic printing, November 2009

Design by Katrina Damkoehler
Text set in Administer

For Tavish, Tory, and Kade

1

CREEPING UP
ON THE KRIKS

Why are so many vampires moving to New York City? It seemed to Maddy that every weekend another van was unloading locked coffins, crystal chandeliers, velvet drapes, and twine-wrapped packages marked FRAGILE—GOBLETS or ANCIENT MAPS—DO NOT BEND. Of course, it's hard to spot true nightcrawling, bloodsucking vampires from your basic nightcrawling, strange neighbors, like the ones who just moved across the street from the Livingstone family. As Maddy knew, a good spy has to keep an eye out for clues.

"I wish the von Kriks would *do* something." Maddy was kneeling on the family room window seat, watching the von Krik townhouse through her binoculars.

"You need a better hobby than spying." Hudson, at age nine, was two years younger than Maddy but stood eye-to-eye with her, which made him bossy. Hudson was also intensely gorgeous, and so the Livingstone family's no-mirrors rule was especially hard on him.

"Unless it's naked people," piped up thirteen-year-old Lexie from under the card table. "Cavorting nudes would be compelling, spywise." Lexie knew hard words like *cavorting* and *compelling* because she was poetic.

Maddy, who was not gorgeous and not poetic, but

very bold, focused the lens. "The man's got popcorn. The woman is knitting."

"Knitting's a useful hobby. As long as you don't give homemade scarves for Christmas." Hudson snapped a piece of the Caspian Sea into his jigsaw puzzle. Hudson loved puzzles. Whenever he finished one, he put it in the freezer. Since none of the Livingstones ate frozen foods, it was perfect storage space.

" 'And if my stocking hung too high, / Would it blur the Christmas glee, / That not a Santa Claus could reach, / The altitude of me?' " quoted Lexie, who loved the words of doomed poets. Today she was dressed in white, in tribute to doomed poet Emily Dickinson, as she held her breath and reenacted the tragic drowning death of doomed poet Percy Bysshe Shelley. This game always dragged on too long, since Lexie could hold her breath indefinitely.

"Purebloods like to sleep in extra darkness. Betcha that's why those Kriks stashed their coffins under the dining room table." Just saying the word *coffins* made Maddy's teeth sharpen. She had never slain a vampire before—not in the Old World and certainly not in this one. But the urge had been passed on to her, which made her different from the rest of her family. For example, she was the only Livingstone who drank a morning mug of tomato or pomegranate juice, pretending it was fresh blood. Her parents worried, but Maddy knew her instincts would be helpful one day.

Meantime, spying on the von Kriks seemed like exciting practice.

"Those aren't coffins," corrected Hudson. "They're

valuable Victorian clothes trunks. You've got vampires on the brain. Any of our species is quite rare. There are fewer of us than peregrine falcons or southern sea otters." He sniffed. Hudson was proud of his lineage.

Maddy knew the real problem was that neither Crud nor Hex—as she sometimes called her brother and sister— minded a rainy puzzles-and-poets afternoon. But Maddy was edgy with energy. "Idea! Let's use our ancient family skeleton key to break into the von Krik house."

"Bad plan, Mad." Hudson sighed. "If the Kriks aren't vamps, all you've done is bothered two nice people on their weekend. But on the chance they *are*, a pure vampire bloodline is stronger than our fruit-bat, vampire-hybrid mix. They'd eat you alive, which would pretty much ruin Valentine's Day."

"And don't forget." Lexie rolled out from under the table. "If you angered a couple of purebloods and they caused a commotion, the Argos would make us leave town."

"Yeah, yeah, yeah." Mention of the Argos always irked Maddy. In her four years in this city, she'd never met one single Arg face-to-face, and she only half believed that these stealthy New World peacekeepers kept constant check on pureblood and hybrid behavior.

"And if we're exiled, how would Mom and Dad find jobs they like as much as dog walking? Or find a rock band to play in as cool as the Dead Ringers?" Lexie continued. "Don't forget, New York orthodontists are the best."

"Think about it, Mads," added Hudson, bossy as usual.

Maddy didn't want to think about it. Of course Crud and Hex would say those things. First, because no student in the history of P.S. 42 Elementary got as many valentine flowers and chocolates as handsome Hudson. Second, Lexie was very worried that, despite her new braces, her adult fangs would stay snaggly forever.

Maddy kept spying. The man picked popcorn off his sweater. The woman squinted at her knitting, which looked suspiciously scarf-ish. "If I slayed them—in self-defense, of course," Maddy clarified, "then the name Livingstone would go down in history."

Hudson snorted. "We've been around almost four hundred years. It's *already* down in history."

"You better not bug them," said Lexie, rolling back under the table. "The Argos see all."

Maddy dropped her binoculars. "Later, blisters. I got some spying to do."

Lexie's drowning hand rippled good-bye. Hudson snapped in another puzzle piece and softly cheered himself on.

The rarely used skeleton key was hidden by the front door underneath the never-ever-used phone book. Maddy pulled it out and stared at the engraved name Lvyngstone, then sniffed its rust-encrusted scent. The key was a relic from the Old World, a place her parents rarely spoke of since the Night of the Flight to Manhattan four years ago, a swift departure for reasons not fully understood—at least not by Maddy. What she did know was that the Old World had become increasingly dangerous with pureblood predators, and unsafe for families such as the Livingstones. In escaping to the neutral terrain of the New World, the Livingstones had traded the carnivorous privilege of eternal life in order to become a normal New World family and to age naturally.

For the most part, the New World was an improvement on the Old. For one thing, time flowed faster. So now Maddy got one year older per year, instead of per century. That meant she celebrated real birthdays, with candles and kazoos and new sneakers for her ever-lengthening feet.

But not all had worked out as planned. The Night of the Flight was also the last time that Maddy'd had use of her night wings. They'd disappeared the moment she'd touched down in New York. Sometimes, she could feel the itch between her shoulders, and it made her wistful. And if life was more peaceful here, it was also more secretive. For example, every day, Maddy had to pretend to be a regular, human eleven-year-old girl instead of an ancient, fruit-bat vampire girl. Every night, she did peculiar things such as brush her teeth and sleep on a feather mattress instead of swooping over moonlit fields in search of plump mice to bite.

And then there was her urge. Crud and Hex didn't have Maddy's bloodthirsty passion for sniffing out nightwalkers. In the apartment elevator, she jammed on her mother's sunglasses and tucked her three essentials—pencil, notebook, and asthma inhaler—deep into her pocket.

Outside, rain had made the city soggy. It dripped from awnings and raincoats and umbrellas.

"Hi, Maddy! Tell your parents I got a fresh haul of grape-fruit and guava this morning." Big Bill, the owner of the Candlewick Café, was unloading a crate of vegetables from a truck parked curbside.

"Okay."

A Japanese water beetle was crawling alongside a cucumber crate. Instantly Maddy's tongue shot out and snapped the bug into her mouth. Juicy, with a twist. Yum. She spat its jumbly leftovers over her shoulder, then cast Bill a guilty look. What if he'd been watching? Nobody liked to see girls eat bugs, or spit out bug parts. But it was so rare to find a ripe beetle in winter.

It wasn't an accident that the Livingstones' apartment was twelve flights up from the Candlewick Café, a popular health food restaurant. Vampires, even vegan hybrids such as the Livingstone family, have strong and demanding thirsts. Seeded fruits are the staples of a healthy fruit-bat diet, and were served daily at the Candlewick, where the Livingstones kept an account. Still, sometimes Maddy could not resist a crawly creature. Only sometimes, though.

The von Kriks had just moved into the biggest townhouse on the block. Its tombstone-thick gray walls were surrounded by an arrowhead-spiked gate and guarded by stone gargoyles. The lion-head door knockers looked real enough to roar, but there was also a side entrance. Maddy checked that Big Bill was not on the lookout before she swooped down the alley.

The skeleton key worked like a charm. In the next moment Maddy was crouched in the von Krik pantry. Her heart pounded. She loved being a sneaker-upper and hider-inner almost as much as a spying-onner. Her ears picked up the sound of clacking knitting needles. Her extra-sharp nose caught a whiff of burnt popcorn.

Back in the Livingstone apartment, the others continued talking to Maddy by echolocation.

"Watercolors might be another good hobby for you, Mads," said Hudson. "You're not too bad at art."

"It is *so* rude to enter a house uninvited," added Lexie. "Especially a vampire home. That's a sure way to annoy them."

Maddy pushed up her sunglasses and bounced back a message. "Stalking Old World nightwalkers is more important than listening to your nerdy advice." If vampires lived in this house, Maddy wanted to know about it. Just because she was small and had mild asthma didn't mean she wasn't crafty.

She whipped out her notebook and pencil. Time for the official prowl.

"Glamorama!" she whispered. From the chessboard marble front hall to the gold-gilded parlor, each huge, creaky room dwarfed its old-fashioned furnishings. Was this a clue? Vampires always inherited deeds and property, but rarely held cash or credit cards. Which was why they tended to stick with the inherited, antique decor.

Old, Maddy jotted, because she wasn't sure about the spelling of *antique*. Her hyperextended tongue quickly check-licked the marble mantelpiece—dusty. Then she got down on all fours and licked the jewel-toned carpet—musty.

Maddy

She picked a vase off the grand piano and let her tongue roll down to touch bottom. No clues, but it had a nice dried-water, mushroomy taste. She jotted:

Not clean.
No silver.
No modern art.
Madison Madison Madison

This last notation was not a clue, but Maddy really liked to write her name. In the dining room the drapes were drawn and the swimming pool–length table was covered in a stiff cloth. Maddy snapped on a light switch. Nothing happened.

No light.

The pencil slipped from her fingers. She cringed as it rolled along the marble tiles. As she bent to reclaim it, Maddy noticed that her fingernails had shaped themselves into ten clear diamond-hard spears. Of course, all of her defenses were up. Because while plenty of houses contained no silver, no modern art, and some lumpy antiques, almost every home was wired with working electricity.

All homes . . . except for pureblood vampire homes.

Maddy recircled the rooms, her fingers reaching for switches. *Snick, snap, click.* No, no, no. Not a single wattage. Not a flickering pinpoint.

Above, she heard the clomp of von Krik feet across the

carpet. Time to dash. But she'd come so far, she just had to find out more! Maddy darted to the dining room. In a snatch, she whipped back the tablecloth to see the truth she'd suspected all along.

Coffins!

"What is your business here?" The voices were so close and sudden that Maddy shrieked, covering her mouth so her quick-dropped fangs wouldn't show, as she stared into the coldly incredulous faces of both von Kriks.

2

EYES LIKE METEORS

All January, all Lexie had thought about was Dylan Easterby. He was perfection. Of course, she'd always had a tiny crush on him—what girl didn't get a thrill from Dylan? You'd have to be dead. Which, technically speaking, Lexie kind of was. And yet Lexie's crush, always present, always minor, had gone into major upshift now that school had resumed.

During class, she used her fingertip to trace his name in loopy letters along her leg. Occasionally, she caught herself singing "Dylan Easterby" under her breath to the tune of "Oh, My Darling Clementine." At night, Lexie wrapped herself in silky, Dylany dreams. Whenever she thought she was going too batty from her crush, she swore to herself it would fade, much like the suntan Dylan had picked up during the Easterby family's winter vacation to Cancún, Mexico. Once Dylan started peeling, Lexie hoped her crush would peel off, too. Meantime, his skin was so toasted, his eyes so warm, his teeth so straight . . .

"Watch yourself!" Dylan called from across the classroom. Lexie jumped as, with a snap of his thumb and finger, he let something fly.

A silver sparkle caught the air. Lexie heard the object whistling toward her. She clocked its velocity as her hand opened wide to snare it like a Venus flytrap, her instincts identifying that it was inedible, some type of coin. Lexie had the best reflexes in the family, but from the moment she caught the object, she wished she hadn't. It was never a good idea to showcase bat abilities. Too late now. The class had gone berserk.

"Yo!" "See that?" "Lex, you didn't really catch that, whatever it was, in your bare hand, did ya? Didja?"

"It's a peso," Dylan clarified. "From Mexico. Awesome lightning reflexes, Lex."

"More like lucky accident." Lexie shrugged and opened her palm. "Sorry."

"Don't be sorry. Just tell me your secret." Dylan smiled, a row of utterly orderly teeth.

"The secret is that Lexie's got yucky octopus fingers," sniped Mina Pringle with a toss of her head. Kids laughed. Lexie frowned. Mina and Lexie had disliked each other since their first day of fourth grade, four years ago. That was back when Lexie hadn't broken herself of all of her old bat habits, and at recess she'd picked her nose with her tongue. A disgusted Mina had tattled on Lexie, but of course nobody had believed her, and in fact most kids had thought Mina was just being nasty to Lexie on purpose, because she was the new girl.

Mrs. MacCaw, entering the room, rang her cowbell for quiet.

"Yuck-topus," hissed Mina for good measure as she flounced off to her seat.

Lexie hid her hands in her pants pockets. It was true that she had extraordinarily long fingers. Like extra-precise ears and speedy reflexes, hyperextended fingers and toes were a Livingstone family trait. Lexie had never much cared until this second. Now she felt a touch sorry for herself. After all, nobody else at Cathedral Middle School had to deal with being part bat. She kept her fingers under her desk as she peeled her morning orange, sucking in the juice and then storing the seeds in her pocket to give to Hudson.

After homeroom let out, half the class trooped up the stairs for English Literature, while the other half trooped down for World History. Lexie and Dylan were among the down-troopers, but Dylan usually traveled in a large pack of hangers-on. Today he let them go by. "So, Lex, am I ever getting my peso back? 'Cause I'd trade it for the secret of how you caught that coin."

Dylan's eyes were like amber, ocean-rubbed to smoky softness. He used them to look at Lexie as if she were the most important person in the entire school. But Dylan behaved like this with everybody, Lexie reminded herself. That's why he was the best-liked kid in the eighth grade.

" 'Blind eyes could blaze like meteors and be gay,' " Lexie quoted. Dylan looked confused. "That's a line of poetry by Dylan Thomas, who died after drinking himself into a coma," explained Lexie in a rush. "But some people would say he was doomed from the start. Doom catches poets the way other people catch colds."

Dylan laughed in a way that was half friendly, but maybe half scared. "You're an odd duck, Lex," he said. "Go ahead and keep that coin. It's stainless steel, so if you're thinking about getting rich off it, you won't. Sorry."

No more quotes! Lexie warned herself. No matter how doomed you feel. She knew that poems were considered cornball. If only Dylan Easterby wasn't so hypnotic. And don't smile, or your braced-in snag-fangs will show.

So she just nodded, unsmiling, and in the pause, a new pack of friends quickly shuffled up around Dylan, including fellow best-all-around guy Alex Chung, who slapped him on the back. "Did you see the game last night?" he asked. And Dylan, now talking football, melted into the herd.

"Don't even think about it." Mina swooped down and pushed her face so close that Lexie could smell the morning chocolate milk on her breath. It made her stomach churn, since Lexie's own fruit-juice-based blood was lactose intolerant. "Everyone knows I'm taking Dylan Easterby to the Midwinter Social." Mina yawned out more bad milk smell. "In fact, I'm planning to invite him tonight."

Lexie wasn't sure if she had even known about the Midwinter Social.

"And don't pretend like you didn't know about the Midwinter Social." Mina tucked a lemony blond curl behind her ear. "You're too tall and weird for Dylan." She arched an eyebrow. "*Way* too weird, if you ask me. There's something extra creepy about you, Lexie Livingstone. You know it, and I know it."

Although Lexie did not have her night wings anymore, she could feel the danger of Mina's words, and an answering prickle itched at the barely visible wing nubs between her shoulder blades. In another time, she would have hissed in Mina's face and then flown up to the safety of the rafters. Instead, she bared her braces at her foe. "If I were you, Mina, I wouldn't be so quick to judge. So you better watch out, because I might have some new tricks up my nose."

Mina hopped back from Lexie. "Ha, ha, aren't you funny. Just remember—me and Dylan are exactly alike, and in real life, opposites repel. As for your freaky tricks, Lexie, don't you worry. I'll be watching out for them . . ." Her voice was singsong, but her face had a pointy purpose. Then she turned to skim gracefully down the stairs.

Times like this, Lexie wished that her own bat feet did not stick out like a pair of yams. She also wished that Maddy were here at Cathedral Middle instead of across town at P.S. 42 with Hudson. Teeny Maddy intimidated the other kids because she was always up for a brawl. Maddy would never just stand tongue-tied and beet-faced, giving Mina all the flounce-off power.

As Lexie stood there, she noticed a flyer tacked up on the wall:

> **Hey Cathedral Middle!**
> **It's the Middle of Winter**
> **Time for FUN—**
> **Friday Night in the Lunchroom**
> **DRESS for Effect—**
> **DJ Jekyll spins till 10:45 PM**

World History passed in a fog. Lexie flipped her orange seeds and lucky peso over in her palm. Her tense confrontation with Mina had dried up her skin, making it itchy as fleas on sawdust. She needed to take care of that problem, quick. After class, Lexie headed for her locker to spritz herself head to toe from the atomized half gallon bottle of water she kept stored there. Even though their New World skins allowed the Livingstones plenty of freedom to roam both in- and out-doors, they had to be extra careful to keep hydrated, and to wear plenty of moisturizer and sunscreen, even in winter.

As the mist soothed Lexie's skin, new thoughts burned up her brain.

First of all, she decided, no more bat tricks. Watchful Mina was already on high alert. If the Livingstones were ever exposed as nonhumans, the Argos would most certainly exile them from New York. And then where would they go? Certainly not back to the Old World. Unlike her younger brother and sister, Lexie had not forgotten those last treacherous weeks before they'd escaped. She had heard her parents say a thousand times that the Old World was much too dangerous now, and that if worse came to worst, they'd rather end their days on a beautiful beach at high noon, where they'd all stretch out and let themselves crumble to black ash. "The final family crispy cookout," her parents cheerfully called it, trying to make it sound slightly less depressing than everyone knew it was.

Second, but almost just as important—as long as he remained unasked to that Midwinter Social, Dylan Easterby was fair game and he belonged to anyone and everyone. Lexie would not let mini-Mina intimidate her. No way.

And so Lexie's secret scheme began to hatch.

3

NIGHT EXPLORER

Hudson woke up at 4:00 A.M. He always began his day at this moment, and always the same way. First he unzipped himself from the sleeping bag that hung upside down by enforced metal hooks in his closet. Next he stepped out of his pajamas and tucked them under his pillow. Then he squeaked open his bedroom window and climbed out onto the granite ledge, where he stared out over the twinkling city. Lastly, he tucked his head to his chest and let himself drop like a rock.

He gasped at the speed of the twelve-story vertical plunge and then catch as his arms extended, transforming, his body compacting and his wings materializing to take control of the air. What a shame, thought Hudson, so many are denied the joy of night flying. Not his hybrid sisters and parents, whose nocturnal privileges were distant Old World memories. Not his best friend, Duane Rigby, and not his fourth-grade teacher, Mr. Apple. Not even a single member of the NASA space crew.

Though Hudson could not have said why, he knew it was important for him to fly every single night. Not only did it help him keep his basic skills of takeoff, endurance, and landing sharp, but flying gave him a sense of purpose.

Sometimes he liked to imagine that he was in training for something. He was careful about his flights, too, keeping an itinerary of the airplanes landing between 4:00 and 5:00 A.M. Because no passenger wanted to look out an airplane window and spy an oversized, boyish-faced vampire-fruit bat swooping past.

As he arced over Central Park, Hudson's fists uncurled to loosely scatter the family's daily store of seeds. Ninety percent of the seeds wouldn't pollinate, but it was hard for the Livingstones to give up this recycling technique, left over from a time when they'd been more deeply connected to the ecosystem. Then he sped, his reflexes quick to duck a hanging branch or prickly pine or lumpy shadow. In the controlled environment of Central Park, Hudson didn't really have to worry about natural predators. Too bad. A tweak of risk, in Hudson's opinion, would have been intriguing.

Hudson was hardly winded by the time he streaked across Central Park West, heading toward the Hudson River, to which he owed his American name. Familiar smells—garbage, the breeze off the river—directed his path to the lonely wilderness lining the river. Hudson knew his parents would be upset if they ever found out he'd strayed this close to the tip of Manhattan. He himself wasn't sure why he disobeyed them so stubbornly.

"Fly around the park, but that's it, Sport," his mother always reminded him. "Don't chitchat with other species. Home before sunrise, no arguments."

"And if your grades drop, that's it for flight privileges," added his father.

They made rules because they were parents, but his mom and dad never would have vetoed Hudson's nighttime adventures. Just like they didn't prevent Maddy from picking fat ticks off dogs to quench her occasional bloodthirst. Just as they allowed Lexie to reenact tragic deaths. His parents knew Hudson had the most bat in him. He was the only Livingstone who needed to sleep upside down, who communicated with other species, and who could shape-shift for a single, glorious predawn hour into the Old World creature he'd once been.

Hudson had just celebrated his ninth birthday. So far this "ninth" human year had been exceptionally chill. Not just because his class was studying the solar system, or because he was learning to play rock ballads on the piano after centuries of studying Schumann and Mozart. The year's real enchantment, Hudson knew, had everything to do with his odd new friend Orville.

The wild woods stirred strange memories. In the mosses, hostas, and lichen Hudson also caught a whiff of near-forgotten, almost-ancient adventures.

"Over here, Hud." Orville's presence was the faintest echo, hard to find, even for a young bat with saucer ears.

Hudson stretched his wings and zeroed in.

Orville was also some kind of vampire-bat hybrid, possibly part owl or maybe even hawk. He was so old that whatever he'd been was impossible to distinguish from what he was now, all hard black eyes and dirty, crumple-folded wings. Finding a fellow hybrid was so rare that the sight of Orville never failed to fill Hudson with joy. Each night, he half expected to arrive here and find that his friend had long departed.

He crash-landed onto the branch of the spruce where Orville was perched, which caused the creature to squeak in outrage as he rufflingly adjusted himself.

"Pardon me," said Hudson.

"Ah, you fruit bats." Orville wrinkled his nose. "You never can get the hang of a graceful landing. Flying foxes— now those are some elegant pilots. But not fruits."

Hudson shrugged. His claws gripped the branch and he arced to dangle upside down by his knees. As he gave a good post-flight stretch to his muscles, he noticed it.

"What's that weird smell?"

"Pesticide," Orville answered. "They sprayed this morning. Got so warm this month that a few of the hatching cycles have started early, and the young weevils and caterpillars are chewing the seedlings and spruce buds." A peppered moth sputtered by. Orville looked as if he might lunge for it, but at the last moment let it pass.

Hudson kept quiet. In his nearly four hundred years of existence in worlds both Old and New, he had come to appreciate the value of listening. Something big was on Orville's mind. Still, he wasn't prepared to hear the hybrid speak the following words. "Fly with me? I'd like to show you something."

"Okay."

More than okay! Thrilling! Hudson rarely shared flights with Orville, who took his time warming up, cracking his neck and rolling his brittle shoulders. The few times they had flown together, the older creature had led Hudson into wild parts of a natural world Hudson had never seen.

"Stay close," instructed the older bat, and so Hudson hovered on his side as they coasted. Orville acted as tour guide, but sometimes was silent, allowing Hudson to enjoy the night. He inhaled pine and cedar, spied raccoons and porcupines, and followed the bridges and trestles. He let his eye trace the horizons of rock ruins and ravines. Close by, he could hear Orville identify the name of every shrub, possum, cricket, and bird's nest.

Deeper into the woods, Hudson picked up different energy. A whoosh of one creature, then another, flying past. The touch of a wing against his cheek stood Hudson's hair on end.

The night was not as serene as he'd thought. And a lot more crowded.

"Who are they?" Hudson gasped when he and Orville finally circled back and returned to the branch. He could feel his fruit-fortified blood pounding.

"You think you're the only hybrid in this wood?" Orville snorted, then made a point of landing with expert grace.

"Except for you, kind of, yes," Hudson answered truthfully. "Are there many of us?"

"Hard to say. Just like us, they keep themselves hidden," Orville answered. "They bother no one, and nobody bothers them. Young Hudson, I think the time has come for you to sharpen your senses. For example, how would you describe this night?"

Hudson sensed it was the wrong answer when he said, "Great?"

The older bat tipped his head. "What else?"

"Uh . . . fast, chill—"

"Chill!" Orville hopped. "Chilly, exactly. But not frosty. And what month is it?"

"January." Hudson was perplexed. He'd meant *chill* as another word for "great." Kids at school were always using that word. Hudson was proud when he picked up on slang—usually he hardly ever noticed it.

Orville sighed. "Did you know that our globe is heating up because humans use too much energy? Excess gases become trapped in the atmosphere. The trapped gases are overheating the planet. They melt our glaciers and confuse our forests. Our entire ecosystem is getting sick."

"We're studying the *solar* system right now," said Hudson primly. "The ecosystem isn't until April." He didn't like to be ignorant, and he had not known about the trapped gases. So it seemed important to explain why.

Orville's eyes were hard as a burnt match. "You are special, Hudson. You're a pure link between the human and animal world."

Hudson preened. Privately, he'd always thought he was a particularly spectacular morph of bat and boy. He wished he could brag to more people about that. Or any people, come to think of it. "Thanks."

"That's why it is important that you know."

Hudson drew sharply alert. "Know what?"

"It might be that you have been chosen, Hudson. New World creatures have been waiting for a young protector. I'd always thought it was a rumor whispered among hybrids to comfort themselves, but with our woods in crisis, I must admit, I'm hopeful."

Now Hudson wasn't sure if he wanted to preen some more or fly away. His stomach churned. A protector? Him? He'd never protected anything in his life. In fact, he still hid upside down in his closet during thunderstorms.

Orville continued, "According to legend, the Protector defends the One, but helps the Many."

"I don't get it. Who's the One? Who's the Many?" Hudson wondered why he couldn't get to be the One instead of the Protector. It seemed chiller to be the One.

"I'm sorry, but I don't have all your answers. What I hope I have shown you is our dilemma." Orville's thin wings opened as if to hug the entire landscape.

Hudson nodded solemnly. "What can I do?"

"To the true activist, the question becomes 'What can't I do?' "

A quiet rush of purpose stood Hudson's ears on point and woke up his whole body. Here it was—that tweak of risk, that sliver of dare he realized that he had been waiting for all these sleepless, urgent nights.

Orville wanted him to protect these creatures.

Was Hudson ready?

4

KILLER INSTINCT

It had been nearly a week, but Maddy still had to puff a couple of times on her inhaler whenever she thought of those von Krikity eyes on her.

When she'd shrieked, they had recoiled. A good bat shriek is tough on the ears.

"What, exactly, do you think you're doing?" The woman had pointed a knitting needle like a knife to stab Maddy in the heart, while the man had held up his popcorn bowl like a rock to drop on her head.

"Nothing." Untrue. But "vampire hunting" seemed like an unsafe response.

"You are a small girl. Perhaps eleven years old." The woman, who spoke in a strange accent, was very tall and thin, with shiny brown hair and a smoothly sculpted face that made it hard to know how old she was.

"You sneaked into our house." The man was also very tall, but pale, with eyes as coldly blue as arctic sky.

"Yes," Maddy confirmed. "But I didn't mean you any harm," she qualified, though she wasn't sure if this was true.

"Were you planning to rob us?" asked the woman.

"No." True.

"Do you want something from us?" asked the man.

"No." Untrue. Obviously, she wanted to know if the von Kriks were vampires. And, if so, could they sense that she was a hybrid? Did they consider Maddy an enemy, as they would have in the Old World? Maddy sometimes missed those Old World days, hiding from the magnificent pure-bloods, who were expert hunters and fliers and a terrifying menace to all other populations.

"Would you like some puffed corn?" asked the man.

Maddy raised an eyebrow. *Puffed* corn? Sometimes ex-Old World nightwalkers messed up their vocabulary. It was a problem when you outlived slang. But maybe "puffed corn" was the right expression wherever he was from. Maddy took one to be polite, but her skin tingled with suspicion.

"Whatcha got there?" she asked, pointing under the table.

"Oh, that's where we're storing our Victorian clothes chests," explained the woman, "until we find the right place to display them."

Victorian clothes chests? A pox on old Crudson, thought Maddy, for being right again.

"Where do you live, little girl?" asked the man.

Maddy stuck up her chin. She hated being called little, especially when she was feeling so predatory. "Across the street, twelve flights above the Candlewick Café."

The von Kriks shuddered. Vegetarian cuisine wasn't for everyone.

"Which means I'm your neighbor," said Maddy, "and

since the door was open, I came over to introduce myself. I'm Madison Livingstone."

"Our door is never open," said the woman at the same time the man said, "We are Nigel and Nicola von Krik. How exciting for us to meet a fresh new neighbor."

Maddy thought she saw Nicola frown at her husband.

"And you are a . . . human being?" asked Nicola.

"Of course. One hundred percent." Untrue, but Maddy was surprised. Her human beingness had never been questioned before. Was she imagining things, or had Nigel just licked his lips?

"Our servant, Snooks, is preparing a late-afternoon snack of steak tartar," said Nicola. "Why don't you join us—neighbor?"

A stern voice in Maddy's head reminded her that she had already had her beetly pinch of protein for the day. Luckily, the voice was too small to pay attention to. "Sure."

As peculiar as the von Kriks were, they were also charmingly polite. In the dining room, Snooks served up porcelain plates of raw, chopped meat. Maddy had never tried steak tartar before. On first taste, her stomach and memory rumbled like a waking volcano. This was the most delicious dish she'd ever sunk her fangs into. It reminded her of long, long ago, way back when she was pure human. And the von Kriks' crystal water goblets made her feel as if she were a guest at a splendid dinner party. The von Kriks seemed to be enjoying their tartar, too. They cleaned their plates in no time.

"The cuisine is the best part of being here, my dove," murmured Nicola.

"I couldn't agree more, my darling," said Nigel.

It was a known fact that a reformed pureblood could eat anything the New World had to offer. With a reporter's stealth, Maddy took out her notepad and pencil and hid them on her lap.

"You have foreign accents. What country are you from?" Maddy asked.

"We don't have accents," said Nigel at the same time that Nicola said, "London?"

Liars, Maddy wrote. "What brings you to New York City?"

"Business," said Nicola as Nigel said, "Pleasure."

Maddy added an exclamation mark to *Liars!*

"What are you writing?" asked Nicola.

"I want the recipe for steak tartar," Maddy said.

"Raw steak," said Nigel.

"And a chopping knife," added Nicola. "That's it. Please put away your book."

After lunch, the von Kriks took Maddy on a tour of their grand home, which included a music salon and a portrait gallery.

"Are you tired?" asked Nigel. "You can leave anytime. As in, now."

"Not yet, thanks." Maddy could tell the von Kriks were uncomfortable in her presence, mostly by the way Nigel twitched while Nicola chewed on a bead of her exquisite jet bead necklace.

Maddy smiled, attempting to look friendly.

"As in, *now*," repeated Nicola. "Snooks will show you out."

"In a minute." Were they always so rude to guests? Or was it her? Maddy knew she had a tendency to be a bad guest. Like at sleepovers, when she couldn't resist overscaring other girls with her moment-by-moment reenactment of Marie Antoinette's gory death. But Maddy had been there—an eyewitness in the crowd.

"Who are all these portraits?"

"Beloved ancestors," said Nigel at the same time that Nicola said, "Just some old dead people." And now it was Nigel who frowned at his wife.

"Where are the portraits of you?" Maddy quirked an eyebrow. The undead were not allowed to have their images reproduced or displayed. It was a rule that did not change, no matter which World you were in. No photographs, no portraits—now that would be a sure sign.

"Snooks sent them out for cleaning," said Nigel at the same time that Nicola said, "Oh, up in the attic."

Maddy's fingernails pricked. *Lying pureblood vampires!*

"Eeeeeee—Madison! Get home right this instant and set the table." Maddy's mother had suddenly echolocated her in a sonic blast that made Maddy jump.

"Gotta dash, but I'll be back," Maddy promised. She grabbed her coat and prepared to flee.

"Finally! And the door is always locked, neighbor," said Nicola at the same time Nigel told her, twitchingly, "Next time, *we* will visit *you*."

27

• • •

Except that they didn't. Over the next few days, Maddy trained her binoculars so often on the von Krik house that she thought her eyeballs would pop out. She even spied from bed, though her window view picked up just a shadowy triangle of the portrait gallery, where neither von Krik cared to tread.

"And they do everything by candlelight, and they don't have television," Maddy mentioned a few nights later during a family supper when the subject of the von Kriks came up—which it often did, since this was her favorite subject, by far.

"The whole point of moving to the New World is that you no longer want to hunt or be hunted," said Hudson. "You've really got to leave those poor Kriks alone so they can get on with their noneternal lives."

"If they're here in peace, they should want to be friends," argued Maddy. "We could talk about the Old World days."

"Even if you get nostalgic for those times, others might not feel the same way," Hudson argued back. "I, for one, hate to be reminded about how we stayed immortal. Especially now that I've gone vegan. No wonder they're hiding from you, Maddy."

" 'You say you love; but with a smile / Cold as sunrise in September,' " piped up Lexie.

Maddy frowned. Were Nigel and Nicola hiding from her? How would she slay them if they didn't even want to be friends?

"We're hearing a lot of glum quotes from you these days, Lex." Their father stood at his end of the table, carving up the watermelon. "Let's try to liven things up here. How about we play our new demo, and you kids tell us what you think?" He and their mother had just returned from band practice, which always put them in a cheerful mood.

Their mom cranked up the new Dead Ringers tune on the sound system as the others eagerly passed their plates around, but the mushy pink fruit soured Maddy's appetite. Now that she knew the pleasure of raw steak, raw steak was all she wanted.

Grainy watermelon could not compete. She pushed her plate away.

Lexie was only licking at her fruit, too.

Their mother was a wise old bat who missed little. Her nose ring glinted as she turned to appraise each daughter. "Here's one girl with feverish eyes and another with feverish cheeks. If I didn't know better, I'd say you're both in love."

"Ah, love." Their father smiled. "Children, mark the last day of February on your calendar. That's your mother's and my three hundred ninety-fifth wedding anniversary. We're planning a big party."

"1612. Such a romantic year." Their mother batted her spiky eyelashes.

"Ick." Hudson spat a seed into his napkin. "Parents in love."

"Ick," Maddy agreed. Though Maddy didn't know anyone else's folks who were in such perfect harmony as hers.

Then again, nobody else had parents who wore matching black nail polish and could charge such huge fees at Wander Wag, their dog-walking service, because all dogs were so obedient under their instinctive care.

Lexie was quiet. After kitchen cleanup, she excused herself to bed. Maddy swooped to every window, spying on each angle of the von Krik house. She attempted echolocating them—if they were bats, especially vampire bats, surely they'd lob over an answer, it was only good manners. But her messages diluted like mist into the void.

Defeated, Maddy performed her nightly chore, filling all twenty-two of the apartment's humidifiers that cooled the air and kept the family's thin skin from drying out while they slept. Then she dropped off her daily store of seeds with Hudson before joining Lexie in their shared bedroom, where she found her sister winding her hair into sponge rollers.

"What are you doing?"

"Mina Pringle has beautiful curly hair. She's my opposite, which probably means she's irresistible." Lexie sighed. "Tell me what I look like, Maddy. Be honest, but lyrical."

"Let's see. Your eyes are dreamy, brown as bittersweet chocolate. Your hair is black as wet tar. Your ears poing out like Mom's. Your nose squinks up like Dad's."

"That's how you look, too," said Lexie. "Except that you're really short, with a chin like a spade, and your eyes are too wide-awake for dreams."

"Hudson's the hottie," Maddy conceded. "You're a fraction cuter than I am, maybe, but most people have to get to know us to like us. And I personally think that Hudson's *too* handsome. People's knees shake when he walks by."

Lexie bolted another sponge onto the top of her head. "I only want one pair of knees to shake when I walk by."

"Oh, yeah? Whose?"

Her sister wilted against the headboard and made a woeful clickity sound in her throat. Maddy hadn't heard Lexie make that noise since their last visit to Père-Lachaise cemetery in Paris, when she visited the grave of doomed rock poet Jim Morrison.

Now Lexie gave Maddy a whole earful of Dylan Easterby, including the peso story and Mina's threat. "So I hatched a secret scheme," Lexie ended.

"Which is?"

"I texted Dylan a poem inviting him to the Midwinter Social."

"Wow. Great secret scheme." Untrue. Most kids did not like poems. In fact, Maddy knew only one kid who did, and her name was Lexington.

"Do you want to read it? It's an original sonnet."

"Maybe later. Did Dylan text you back?"

Her sister squirmed. "Not yet."

Maddy thought. "Idea. When you're around Dylan, do more peso-catching. I think it's the bat stunts that spark him up more than the sonnets."

"Bat stunts? No way. Mina's way too watchful. I'll have to rely on my regular human-y charms. Besides, acting batty goes against everything Mom and Dad always say. Remember, the Argos could be anywhere, watching to make sure we don't show off."

Maddy flicked her bladed fingers. She'd heard it all a hundred times before. In her opinion, the Argos sounded like another one of her parents' scare tactics, like the one they told the kids about how watching too much TV would make them go blind.

Once Lexie had settled into her Dylany dreams, Maddy stole out to the family room, where she found her Magic Markers and her parents' shirt cardboards that they saved from the dry cleaner's. Maddy's parents liked to wear their T-shirts starch-pressed so that people could easily read the advertisements silk-screened onto them. The ads were either for Wander Wag, the Dead Ringers, or the Candlewick, depending on their mood.

All night, Maddy worked, right until she heard Hudson get up.

The next day was perfect with a cloudless, chilly sunshine. As soon as school let out, Maddy headed to the von Krik house. She gave a courtesy knock before using the skeleton key to let herself in.

The von Kriks were slumped together in their darkened den playing backgammon. As soon as she saw Maddy, Nicola started to suck on her necklace beads.

"Ahoy, neighbors," Maddy chirped. "Miss me?"

"Of course not. We've been terribly busy," said Nicola at the same time that Nigel said, "Little Madison, how did you get into our house?"

"The door was open. Look, I brought gifts." Maddy

held up her shirt-cardboard portraits—one for each Krik.
She was very happy to see that the cardboards truly cap-
tured the Kriks' likeness. So she was hurt by Nicola's
next question.

"Who are these people?" Nicola's voice was thin
with mistrust.

"Surprise! They are you." Maddy waved the cardboards
closer. "I drew you each a portrait."

At that, both von Kriks hissed. Their spindly hands covered their faces. "You made us so ugly," whimpered Nigel.
"So old. Worse than our portraits in the attic!"

"Old and ugly? Not at all. Look again, in the natural
light." Maddy knew that purebloods were a hundred times
more sensitive to light than hybrids. She ran to a window
and yanked open the dusty drapes. Sunlight flooded in.
She held up the portraits again.

The von Kriks writhed. Nigel dropped to the ground.
Nicola hid her face with a pillow. "Close the drapes!"

"What's the matter?" As if she didn't know.

"We're allergic to sunshine!" Nigel kicked his brittle
legs.

"We have polymorphic light eruption disorder!" Nicola
wrung her bony hands.

"Sunshine is loaded with vitamin D. It'll make you feel
so good." Maddy cackled. "Should I bring you some water?
You're both looking a touch dehydrated." She allowed herself another tiny cackle. A light-headedness was beginning
to fill her head, a wonderful feeling that she had experienced as a hybrid in the Old World the first time she'd

too enthusiastically bitten and slayed a wild duck. That had been a splendid night, a feast for all. For most fruit hybrids, slaying was extremely distasteful work, even for the tiny amount of blood they needed to stay eternal. But not for Maddy. After that duck, Maddy had taken over the family hunting—of mice, rats, birds, and once even a deer. Maddy never imagined that she could possibly feel quite so untamed again as that breathless night in the Old World.

Until now.

Now Maddy watched as Nigel rolled under the sofa. Nicola was coughing up phlegm. Both von Kriks were moaning and wheezing and looked to be extremely uncomfortable. She knew she should stop holding up the portraits, but the von Kriks seemed to bring out her most deadly, secret slayer's instinct.

"Ahem!"

Maddy whipped around. Uh-oh. Snooks. And by the grim look in his lizard eye, Maddy knew he'd figured out she meant the von Kriks nothing but real harm.

5

MASK OF NIGHT

Dylan finally answered Lexie's text sonnet with one line. It was not yes. It was not no.

It was: **LEX U R XLNT**.

By then, everyone knew that Dylan Easterby and Mina Pringle were going to the Midwinter Social. Together.

Whenever Lexie thought about her dumb sonnet, she wanted to drop and roll and roll until she'd rolled herself under a rock, where she would then live out the rest of her human life as a love-spurned hermit.

Dylan's kindness only added to her misery. Like the way he always called out "Hey, L.L.," in homeroom. Or, when he was standing beside her in chemistry lab, "Look, I'm nexty Lexty." Or when, after lunch, he'd offered her a section of his tangerine. "And all my tangerine seeds, too. I know you collect 'em." The crowning humiliation was when Dylan downloaded Lexie's phone number with her own personal ring tone from a Dead Ringers tune.

"He just did that because he pities me," Lexie confided to her best friend, Pete Stubbe. "He thinks I'm an oversized octopus."

"More like you're overreacting. No doubt Mina asked Dylan to the Social first, and Dylan said yes because he's a gentleman, not a cad." Pete's deep yellow eyes and thick thatch of silvery blond hair gave him an unusual look. This, plus his shyness, caused most kids to keep their distance from him. To Lexie, though, Pete was good old Pete, who always saved her a seat, and who loved famous duels as much as Lexie loved doomed poets. They'd been best friends for years, even though Pete's parents, Mr. and Mrs. Stubbe, didn't like Lexie, no matter how polite she was to them.

" 'I look at the hand you held, and the ache is hard to bear,' " Lexie quoted, even though Dylan had never held her hand.

"You and I could go to the social together," Pete said, his voice cracking. These days, Pete's voice tended to pitch like a ship in the high seas, rolling low one moment and squeaky high the next. Right now it was squeaking, and he didn't seem too happy about it. "If nothing better comes up for you, that is."

"Thanks." Lexie hoped her smile didn't look as dreary as she felt. Maddy's advice niggled at her. If she'd acted battier, would she have won Dylan's heart? Would she have shaken his knees? Was it too late for tricks?

Wednesdays after school, karate class was in the gym. Lexie had a passion for karate, and not just because Dylan and his friends took it. In the Old World, self-defense meant either a well-placed bite or a speedy takeoff. But karate called for real New World–y skills, as taught by their very cool music teacher, Ms. Katz—Sensei Katz during class—who was a black belt.

On Wednesday, Lexie walked into the gym (or dojo, as it was called during karate hours) to find Mina and her friend Lucy encamped in the stands. Lexie frowned. These days Mina seemed to follow Dylan everywhere, clinging like a staticky sock to his smallest activity.

Centuries change, mused Lexie, but drippy girls never do.

Lexie waved to Pete, who was also in the bleachers and reading his favorite book, *The Three Musketeers*. Then she took her place on the mat. She ignored Mina, though she bet her lemonheaded enemy was laughing over Lexie's long feet.

Sensei Katz stood in front and led the class creed. "I seek to adjust to every situation, good or bad, which I may meet in my daily life!" Lexie usually shouted this motto to get her energy up. Except this afternoon, with Mina watching from above, her voice sounded whispery-crickety in her own ears—which she imagined poinging out like teacup handles through her knife-flat black hair.

"Let's start with side thrust kicks," instructed Sensei.

"Eee-ah!" Dylan kicked one out right then. Not good, but a bunch of kids clapped anyway.

From somewhere in the city, Maddy had located Lexie and was bouncing a message: "Do it, Wimpus Leximus. Don't worry about the Argos—I'm sure they have better things to do than hang out at beginner karate class. How about trying the ol' knee trick?"

The knee trick was an easy one because all the Livingstones' knees bent both backward and forward. Nothing special, unless you were a pureblood human. Then it might be considered a feat.

Lexie caught Dylan's eye. Though he was far away and surrounded by his usual posse, he saw her and smiled. Oh, those teeth. Not a snaggly one in the bunch. Yes, she'd do it! A knee trick was essentially harmless. And on the remote chance an Arg was creeping around the dojo, looking for a hybrid crime, Lexie would simply explain that her knee had popped by accident.

Lexie tried to echolocate Maddy, but her sly sister had moved off.

"*Ichi, ni, san, shi,*" Lexie counted in Japanese, winding up her nerve as she waited her turn. Her knees had not bent backward in so long that she cringed to hear them crack as she rotated.

On Lexie's turn, Sensei Katz pointed. "*Ki-ai!*" Lexie shouted. Her knee jerked, under-dipped, and pivoted, the heel of her foot brushing her nose as she twisted into a whip-smooth side thrust kick that she retracted so quickly, it might not have even happened, except that it did.

Anyone who saw it burst into wild finger-pointing and whoops. Those who hadn't jumped up and down and demanded to know what they'd missed.

Sensei Katz was at Lexie's side in a flash. "Okay, Lexington, don't move. Can you feel approximately where it snapped? Can you indicate the fracture?"

"I don't think I fractured anything." Through lowered eyes, Lexie stole another quickie look at Dylan, who appeared positively awestruck.

Now Sensei was kneeling and tapping a finger to Lexie's knee. "You're not in . . . tremendous pain?"

"No, not really. See, I'm double-jointed in both my knees."

"Yeeks," said Sensei. "So you are." She looked a touch afraid. She tapped Lexie's knee a couple more times before she straightened up and shook her head wonderingly. "Don't do that again, okay? I'm liable."

"That was wild," said Dylan. But he seemed sparked, just as Maddy had promised. "Cripes, Lex. Just thinking about your knees makes mine hurt."

"Yow, I wish I was double-jointed," said Alex.

"And could catch a peso at the speed of sound," added Dylan.

"No, the peso was only traveling at a rate of thirty-seven miles per hour," Lexie corrected. The guys looked impressed.

Lexie could feel Mina fuming in the stands. Worry gnawed the pit of her stomach. Mina was sharper than the other kids. If anyone was onto the fact that Lexie had performed a humanly impossible feat, it was Mina.

When Pete caught up with Lexie afterward to walk her home, he seemed less astonished. As in, not at all. His yellow eyes were coolly disapproving, and he didn't acknowledge Lexie's showstopping kick. Not that Lexie expected him to—but she didn't think Pete needed to keep his nose stuck in *The Three Musketeers* for the whole walk, either. Of course, Pete had always been protective of her, to the point where sometimes Lexie wondered if he knew her secret. Other times, she suspected Pete was a fellow hybrid, too—though her friend was much too discreet to reveal an Old World connection.

"Are you mad?" she asked as they turned the corner to her apartment.

Out poked Pete's nose. "More like alarmed. No love is worth breaking your knees over."

"Come on, don't be grouchy—I know, let's pit stop at Candlewick for a Garden of Diva fruit blend, with a scoop of bee pollen," Lexie bribed. "We can put it on our house account."

"Some other time. Bye, Lex. See ya tomorrow."

Lexie watched Pete go. He was probably right. Love was driving her crazy, and Pete was a voice of reason. On the other hand, Lexie speculated, if every person in the world listened to their voices of reason, there probably wouldn't be a single poem.

But love was scary. Love made doomed poets jump overboard cruise ships, or drink poison, or stick their heads in ovens.

For poetic bat types, there were different rash options.

"I can't waste another night dreaming about Dylan," Lexie told her sister later that evening as she changed into a tracksuit, no sneakers, and stuffed some clothes into her bed to make a Lexie-sized lump. Unlike Hudson, the girls did not have special outdoor night-flight privileges, since neither of them could transform. But that didn't mean they weren't skilled. "It's time to take action. I'll be gone an hour, maybe more. I need to get downtown and profess my love."

Maddy's eyes widened. "Are you for real?"

" 'Reality is wrong. Dreams are for real.' " Lexie quoted the words of doomed rap poet Tupac Amaru Shakur, whose very name was a poem Lexie liked to recite. "You've got to cover for me, sis."

"No problem. Got your back. I'm your number-one co-conspirator. I'll never squeal. My word is gold." Maddy was always happy when people other than herself were breaking rules.

After their parents had gone to bed, and with Maddy standing guard, Lexie swung out the window, inching her way to the fire escape, which she took down to the sixth floor, the best point from which to plunge. While Lexie had not been blessed with Hudson's shape-shifting powers, she did not have his clumsiness, either. In fact, she possessed amazing night stealth. Under the cover of darkness, Lexie was strong as a bodybuilder and agile as a trapeze artist. She could hurdle fences, swing under bridges, run for miles, and roost on the narrowest ledge.

The Easterby family lived downtown on the west side. Lexie had memorized the address a long time ago. One good thing about this city, thought Lexie as she rushed downtown, is that no matter what time of day or night it is, everyone is too busy to look up. Whether rushing across town for dinner or uptown to the acupuncturist, people rarely stopped to inhale the polluted air or enjoy the smoggy skyline. And being invisible suits me fine, Lexie decided as she swung and dropped. Since it was so cold, she headed through the theater district. All those bright, hot lights would warm her. Plus, she liked getting a close-up view of the billboards.

At the intersection, Lexie leaped on top of a truck heading south. She made it downtown in minutes. From there it was only a few more vaults to Dylan's apartment complex. She scaled the side of the building, pulling herself up and up and up, until she reached the fourth floor. Slithering around to Dylan's bedroom window of Unit 4F was no problem.

Seeing Dylan was.

"Oooh." Standing in his underwear, Dylan was practicing his side snap and roundabout kicks while his chunky little brother, Charlie, sat on the rug watching him. So much Dylan, all at once, made Lexie realize that spying on a half-naked cavorting person was a very compelling hobby, indeed. Especially if that person was Dylan Easterby.

Lexie pressed her unclipped toenails into the window ledge until she found her balance. She would just peep for a minute. Then leap back down to the sidewalk and toss a few pebbles to his window. When Dylan pushed it open and looked down, that's when she would speak her love— either in lofty verse or regular words, whichever popped into her mind first.

The funny thing about spied-on Dylan was that he didn't seem to be his same, assured schoolkid self. His

face was tense from frowning and his hair stuck sweatily
to his ears as he muttered "coil kick, recoil, recover" along
with his bad kicks.

Oh, no. Had she ever noticed how truly pitiful he was
at karate?

When Charlie gave Dylan's last kick a double thumbs-
down, Lexie started to laugh, promptly losing balance and
pitching backward. Quickly, she veered forward to steady
herself—a little too forward. *Smack!* went Lexie's braces
against the windowpane. Startled, Dylan spun around.
And that was how Lexie found herself staring love-struck
into the wide eyes of the boy she adored, at the same
time Dylan's mouth made a surprised O before shaping
her name. *Lexie?*

Then her footing failed completely. Lexie dropped backward, bull's-eye into a large metal garbage can, a landing
slightly softened by the garbage bags piled up inside.

The window shoved open. Dylan's head poked out.
"Lexie? Lexie! Where are you, Lex?"

"O, Dylan, if thou dost love," whispered Lexie from in
the trash, "pronounce it faithfully." She couldn't help but
tingle—in a way, this was such a feverishly dramatic reenactment of the balcony scene in *Romeo and Juliet*, the most
doomed story of all. "And I, too, have night's cloak to hide
me," she reminded herself. Same as Romeo.

"Stay put. I'll get you out of there." Dylan's head ducked
back inside.

Then Lexie caught a whiff of herself. Not good. Frankly,

stinky. It occurred to her that being rescued out of a large metal garbage can wasn't at all the perfect moment for love-professing.

"Haste, haste," Lexie whispered as she struggled to rescue herself.

"Lex, Lex!" Dylan was already outside. How had he moved so fast?

With a rattling clatter, Lexie tipped over the can. She winced in pain as she stumbled to her feet. Ugh, she was covered top to bottom in slimy bits of apple peel and coffee grounds and eggshell and other goopy scraps of damp, discarded grossness.

"Tupac Shakur," Lexie whispered, for strength. Then she started to run down the alley, as far from Dylan as she could get, and as fast as her long yam feet could take her.

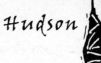

6

PLASTIC POLICEMAN

ECO-FRIENDLY TIPS
REDUCE, REUSE, RECYCLE.
SAVING THE PLANET STARTS WITH YOU!
HOW? MANY WAYS!

- Desist in use of plastic.
- Curb use of dishwasher.
- Wear your garments until they
  start to smell bad—a washing machine
  is a water waster!
- Flush toilet only twice per day.
- Unplug appliances whilst not in use.
  Even plugged in, they suck energy.
- For more information on what you can do to help,
  please visit http://www.stopglobalwarming.org.

MORE TIPS TO COME!!

Hudson stuck his note of tips onto the refrigerator for his entire family to see. He had printed up eighty-nine copies (all on recycled paper, of course) as a gift to the kids at school. He'd decided to put them on the desks of third- through fifth-graders only. Second-graders were too babyish, and sixth-graders were on the scary side. Also, Maddy was a sixth-grader—unanimously considered the scariest sixth-grader of all—and Hudson didn't want her messing with his plan to save the world.

After his night flight with Orville, Hudson had made a decision. If he was destined to be a Protector, he would start immediately. And now that he was training sharper senses on water, air, and land, Hudson didn't like what he saw. The East River, bottomless and brown as cold tobacco juice. The school bus that belched black smoke. The sidewalks an endless concrete trail of mashed gum and blowing litter.

According to Hudson's research, even his own school was a waste pit in dire need of Protection. So now every morning when he arrived at P.S. 42, Hudson snapped off the lights in the boys' and girls' bathrooms. In the administrative office, he unplugged the copiers and scanners and printers and computers. Time permitting, he sneaked into old Mr. Schnur's janitorial closet and cut off the heat generator. Hudson bet the heat heist was his biggest eco-save of all, since it took a couple of hours before the complaints about the cold started up, and at least another hour to find kooky Mr. Schnur, who liked to nap in odd places.

Hudson devoted his after-lunch recess to resorting the brimming trash cans, ensuring that all recycling was in the blue bins, with regular trash in green bins.

"Try all you want, but these kids'll never get their garbage right," Mr. Schnur once commented, leaning over his mop as he watched Hudson work. "I tell 'em over and over. But nobody cares what I say."

This morning, after his usual tasks, Hudson slipped

from classroom to classroom, folding a helpful flyer into each desk. He hadn't signed his name to them, because being a Protector was a selfless act. Hudson's teacher, Mr. Apple, read the tips as he replugged in his computer. "Hudson, my friend," he said cheerfully, "that's got to be your handiwork."

Mr. Apple whistled as he thumbtacked Hudson's tip sheet to the corkboard. Hudson stayed at his desk, silent with hands folded. He even held off scolding a couple of dimwits who had bent their own precious flyers into paper airplanes. At least Duane acted responsibly, studying the list before he tucked it into his notebook binder.

"Thanks, Hud," said Duane.

"Why are you thanking me? How do you know who wrote that list?" asked Hudson.

"The *whilst*," said Duane. "*Whilst* has your name all over it."

Hudson frowned. He hadn't meant to mix an Old World word into his flyer.

He waited for Mr. Apple to tell the class they'd be using first period, Social Sciences, to hold an emergency meeting about the environment. Instead, after roll call and morning announcements, Mr. Apple pointed to the whiteboard.

The word on the board was MEMOIR.

"Can anyone tell me what this word means?" he asked.

Hudson's hand shot up. Mr. Apple picked somebody else. "It means a person's personal history," said the kid.

"Correct, Marcus. And we are going to use the next couple of weeks of Social Sciences to become personal history detectives. Our mission is to track our own life story. Each of you will create a family project and—yes, Hudson?"

"I'd like to remind my classmates that, when writing their life story, to use both sides of their paper."

"Right. Thanks." Mr. Apple's smile turned serious. "So, take a few minutes to consider yourself. For example, where were you born? Have any of you traveled by plane to visit your relatives? Does your family have a secret cabbage soup or fudge brownie recipe that's been handed down for generations? We'll use today to jot down anything we can think of that makes us special.

"We'll put up our finished projects all over the room so that everyone can learn more about our classmates. This'll be cool, I promise."

Hudson didn't wait for Mr. Apple to call on him. "And, class, no oversharpening your pencils. Our trees are precious."

Something smacked his ear and dropped to his feet. Hudson looked down. A spitball. How strange. Hudson knew that spitballs were often aimed at irritating, unpopular, or bizarre students. He had always assumed that his class held him in high regard. He was, after all, extraordinarily handsome, and he had entered fourth grade with many centuries of life experience.

He picked it up. Yes, a spitball, crushed up with slimy spit goo. He wiped his ear, then raised his hand to report it. But Mr. Apple didn't look as though he'd be calling on Hudson again anytime soon.

Hudson checked the room for culprits. Except for Duane, he could never remember the names of any of the young hooligans in his fourth-grade class. He guessed the guilty party was the husky lunkhead sitting behind him on a southwest diagonal.

"Hudson." Mr. Apple's voice was slightly strict. "Eyes on your paper."

Hudson glared at the lunkhead. Using his right hand, he wrote:

MY LIFE, SO FAR
By Hudson Livingstone

I was born at St. Vincent's Hospital, New York City. I am the youngest but not the shortest. I have two bossy older sisters. My mom plays bass guitar and my dad is a drummer for The Dead Ringers. I like fruit. My hobbies are jigsaw puzzles and energy conservation.

He stared at his paper and yawned. This morning, the vanilla-coated facts of his hybrid-human life didn't seem as pressing as what swirled inside his ancient soul. He turned over his paper, now switching to his left hand—bats are ambidextrous—as he began to write his essay again, this time in special Old World calligraphy.

My Life, So Far
By Hudson Livingstone

In the year of 1618, outside the rural province of Pembrokeshire, I was received with great relief and celebration as a firstborn son. Home was a cottage of wattle-and-daub. Father rented cattle and tilled fields of barley. Mother kept goats and tended beehives. Our Bess was a short-jointed mare, fourteen hands high.

Whilst I was yet in milk teeth, an early frost blighted our harvest, followed by a winter so vengeful and bitter we ate naught but winter root and stewed fruit bat. Our misfortune was followed by a deadly scourge of smallpox that—

Hudson broke off. The freckly redhead across the aisle had crumpled up her last paper and was starting on a second, brand-new piece. Usually she was sweet as a peach, and last year she'd given Hudson a pink carnation on Valentine's Day. Too bad she was also a paper-wasting litterbug.

"Attention, freckled redhead girl." Hudson pointed at her. "Both sides, please."

The girl blushed red all over. "Hudson, for the zillionth time, my name's Bethany Finn. And for your information, I did use both sides."

"A doubtful story. Surrender your paper." Hudson held out his hand for it.

Up front, Mr. Apple cleared his throat. "You can't police your fellow students, Hudson. That's my job."

"You might need help at it," said Hudson under his breath.

Mr. Apple had such good hearing, sometimes Hudson

suspected a bit of bat lived in him, too. "Hud, bud, maybe you should spend the rest of this class in the library, where our wastefulness won't disturb you, and where you can concentrate on your notes in peace."

Hudson smarted at the reprimand. He folded his notes and stood. It was a lonely walk to the front of the room. The eyes of the class watched him go.

In the library, he wrote out his secret memoir and read it proudly to himself before tearing it up into a hundred little pieces. It was a spectacular story, with lots of flavor and drama. What a shame that the Argos would never let him go public with it. Time alone in the library gave Hudson new energy to rally the class at lunch period.

"Know this," he decreed as he sat down next to Duane at the table. "Plastic utensils bleed our environment like a stuck boar whose fatal cries of suffering go unheard."

The whole table went very, very quiet.

"Everything you say lately is like a scary warning, Hudson," complained a kid.

Other voices pitched in.

"Yeah, like the lady with the flashlight at the movies if I put my feet up."

"Or the substitute bus driver."

"Or Monsieur Armand, my viola instructor."

"Or my nana if I wake her up from a nap."

"I think Hudson gets the point," said Duane. "But, hey, at least he doesn't try to trade us for his fruit lunch, right?"

Kids laughed—nice laughs, because everyone liked Duane. But Hudson was disappointed nobody asked any questions about plastic utensils. Instead, kids just talked about whether Mr. Apple would choose the indoor gym or outside tarp for after-lunch recess. Hudson quietly chewed his boysenberries. He usually stored the boysenberry seeds in a plastic bag he kept in his—oh, no! Hudson gulped as he looked around. Here he was, lecturing against plastic, when he himself used a new plastic bag every day. How could he be anyone's Protector if he couldn't even protect himself from his own wastefulness?

Down the table, Hudson saw that a lot of other kids were also using cling wrap or the dreaded plastic bags. He stood. "Know this. Every time you use plastics, you are contributing to air pollution."

From the other end of the table, the lunkhead stuck out his tongue. "Hud, know this—every time you opened your mouth today, *you* contributed to air pollution."

Kids laughed—and these laughs didn't sound nice.

"Fie on them," Hudson told Duane later. "I'll protect the planet by myself."

"Sure," Duane said, "but I think you'd have more clout if kids believed you halfway liked them."

Hudson shrugged. "I do halfway like them." Honestly, though, he had never considered them. What did it matter if he liked the kids in his class, halfway or any way? They were, after all, just a bunch of kids.

Four A.M. could not come soon enough. The best part of my day, Hudson decided as he soared into the winter sky. It all goes downhill after that. In some ways, thought Hudson, I'm way better at being a bat than a kid.

When he arrived at Orville's tree, he explained his troubles to him. The sage old hybrid drooped to hear them. "If humans won't be led by a creature as extraordinary—not to mention as handsome—as you, who will rally them to our cause?"

Hudson's voice dropped. "Maybe kids don't see me as a Protector."

Orville scratched a claw gently against the bald crest of his head. "Because you have no clout?"

That word again! Now Hudson had to ask. "What's *clout*?"

"Pull and influence." Orville's eyes were hard black beads. Something stirred in Hudson's memory. Where had he seen those eyes before?

Hudson hunched deeper into his wings. "I am afraid, Orville, that you are correct. I am cloutless."

"Ah, don't take it so hard. It's no matter." They perched for a moment in mutually embarrassed silence. "But perhaps," said Orville slowly, "you might know somebody who does have power, who could show young people the importance of recycling and preserving natural resources, who could help get our message across?"

Hudson thought. The idea seeped in from the edges. A slow idea, because it was somewhat horrifying. Yet, once it had been thought, it could not be unthought. "Well. I might . . . know . . . someone."

7

O HAPPY DAY!

One thing Maddy was sure of—a good bat offense is the best bat defense. Once Snooks had appeared to the von Kriks' rescue, she'd flown at him in a flapping, hissing flurry.

"How dare you call yourself a servant, Snooks, when you haven't cleaned this den in weeks? No wonder you keep these curtains closed!" She'd swooped in closer. "It's like a dust palace in here!"

For a moment, Snooks looked bewildered, but that moment didn't last long enough to permanently damage the Kriks. He shooed off Maddy, lurching over to the velvet drapes and yanking them shut.

The barely conscious Kriks whimpered with relief.

"Little shrimp," said Snooks, wagging a finger right back at Maddy, "you are strange and dangerous." True. The Kriks convulsed in agreement. From beneath the sofa, Nigel's icy eyes were alert as one brittle, waxen hand reached up to grasp Nicola's.

"How do your allergies fare, my darling?" he wheezed.

"Minor hives, my pet. Minor hives." Nicola coughed. "Snooks. Remove her."

Snooks had already hooked a grip under Maddy's collar and was dragging her from the den, down the staircase, and out of the house, where he deposited her with a plop between the smirking doorstop gargoyles. "Don't come back, little shrimp," he said. "You are an unwanted pest. And—" Snooks held up the flat of his palm—*"uninvited."*

Whether he knew it or not, Snooks had cast a spell over his home. Once a vampire has been forbidden from entering the home of an enemy, she cannot intrude under the guise of false friendship. In order for Maddy to cross the von Krik threshold, she would have to announce that she was up to no good. Which, of course, was out of the question.

At least Maddy had her answer. The sunlight test had proven it, she decided. Those von Kriks were bloodsuckers. Even if they were living according to New World rules, their presence was a danger. Who knew when they'd decide they might want to attack their fruit-fortified neighbors? They needed to be driven off, quietly and expertly.

Maddy waited a couple of days before she put the next phase of her plan into action. She used most of her allowance to purchase the ingredients from the grocery store, and walked the whole twelve blocks to St. James Church on Madison Avenue to fill her thermos with the secret kicker ingredient.

Back in the kitchen, Chef Maddy rubbed her hands together. Humming, she tied on an apron and whirled like a windstorm, pulling down bowls and excavating the electric whisk from the cobwebby back of the cupboard.

She stopped a minute to stare down the oven. Since the Livingstones followed an all-raw-foods diet, the oven had never been turned on. Tentatively, Maddy swiveled one knob to BAKE and another knob to 350 degrees. After a few seconds, she opened the oven door and lick-tested the grill—yes indeed, it was warming up nicely. She set two garlic heads onto the oven's top shelf and resumed studying her cookbook. It appeared she would have to improvise in some places.

"For example, instead of using cooling racks, I'll stick them on the counter."

"Stick what?"

Maddy jumped. "Crudson! Get down from there." A pesky squirt of a kid brother was bad enough, but one who could perch from the highest rafters was even worse. "You know Mom says no roosting on the refrigerator."

"And what does she say about hiding icky stuff in the yewn?" asked Hudson.

"First of all, the New World word is not *yewn*, it's *oven*. Second, not that it's your business, but I'm using the oven to bake my delicious white chocolate chip macadamia nut cookies. Now get lost."

"Watercolors would have been a more chill hobby for you." Hudson pinched his nose and made a face. "You're a terrible cook. It smells putrid in here, like . . . like . . ."

"Garlic," said Maddy. "I'm softening two heads. After I peel and chop them, they'll look just like macadamia nuts. Reformed purebloods can't resist gorging on sugary food. But instead, they'll be treated to a sachet of pure garlicky poison." She threw back her head and did her best Count Chocula laugh. Maddy was a big fan of Count Chocula.

"Don't you dare turn on that mixer," said Hudson.

"It's a waste of energy. I'll come down and mix the cookie dough for you by hand." In the next instant, he was off the fridge and standing beside her. He sampled a white chocolate chip. "Blech. Tastes like a dried-up powdered pear, but worse. I'll stick to fruit."

Maddy swatted him away. "And when you're finished mixing, you're going to do another favor for me."

"What?"

"You're going to put on my Elf Scout uniform and sell these cookies to the von Kriks."

"Why would I do that?"

Maddy thought. "Because otherwise tonight while you're sleeping, I'll lock your sleeping bag zipper so you can't get out and fly around, ha ha ha."

"That's called blackmail, Mads."

"That's called you're right, and so what?"

"Well, because it's too wicked. You have to strike a bargain with me, not blackmail me, if you want my cooperation."

Maddy pondered this. Possibly he had a point. Sometimes her darker vampirey instincts did not steer her in the nicest directions. "What's the bargain?"

Hudson whispered it in her ear. Easy enough, and possibly fun, but Maddy acted as though she had to consider it. No use letting Hudson think this was an easy trade. "Mmmaybe."

A smile lit up her brother's face. "O Happy Day!"

" 'O Happy Day' is worse than *yewn* as an Old World expression, Hud," Maddy warned. "You've really got to get with modern vocab. Even *chill* is kind of over." Then

Maddy poured carefully from her thermos. "Substituting some holy water for the egg," she explained. "Watch and learn. And put the thermos back in the fridge—never know when we'll need it again."

"You're not going to really hurt those Kriks, are you? They have as much right to live here as we do."

"That's where you're wrong, Crud. We were here first. We need to protect ourselves. They can go find another neighborhood."

Hudson nodded solemnly. She liked how he was being so attentive.

And she especially liked how he looked all dressed up in her blue Elf Scout uniform once the cookies were cooling and they'd gone to her room to transform Hudson into a girl.

"I don't need a mirror to know I wear this tunic better than you ever did," said Hudson, giving a pretty twirl.

"You wish." But Maddy knew this was untrue. Hudson could wear a laundry bag and look photo perfect, if he could show up in a photo. Maddy yanked up his knee socks and flattened his sash, which had no badges, since Maddy had only been in Elf Scouts for three weeks before she'd been kicked out for biting the troupe's Persian cat mascot, Quincy.

Back in the kitchen, Maddy smoothly slivered open a box of Elf Scouts buttercrumblies. Her parents had bought some boxes last year to be neighborly, then tossed them in the cupboard and forgot about them. Maddy shook out a sleeve of buttercrumblies and replaced them with her own creations. Her cookies looked hunchbacked. Maybe she'd needed that egg after all?

"Good enough," she decided. "Remember, Hud, you'll be selling these buttercrumblies to Snooks. He's the von Kriks' butler, and I'm counting on him to have a sweet tooth, too." She pinched Hudson's cheeks and poofed his hair. "Speak loud and repeat everything Snooks says so I can echolocate."

Hudson looked perplexed. "And you *promise*, if I sell these cookies, that you'll help me with my project?"

"A bargain's a bargain, not a promise. Let's see how much you help me first. Now go. *Go.*"

They left the apartment together. Maddy watched her brother cross the street and knock on the von Kriks' front door before she ducked down the alley and crouched by the pantry entrance, the closest she could get to the Kriks without being inside. She could feel the curse Snooks had set against her hanging thick as a frozen fog around the house. Dang that Snooks and his Unvitation!

"Hello, sir." Hudson's voice was light as meringue. "My name is Henrietta Hudson, and I wanted to know if you'd like to buy some Elf Scout cookies?"

Maddy snickered. Hudson sounded so sweet and innocent. How could Snooks not take the bait?

"Of course you can sample one," said Hudson.

Maddy's fangs gnashed. O Unhappy Day! What kind of dimwit Elf Scout was Henrietta Hudson, anyhow? Offering free tastes was absolutely against Elf protocol. "No samples!" Maddy bounced the words like a punch. Too late.

"Glad you like it," purred Henrietta Hudson. "Elves have been selling reasonably priced, tasty cookies for many years. It's a shame that they insist on using these plastic sleeves, which are a crime against the environment. And now, since you have tried one of these delicious butter-crumblies, you'll have to buy the entire box."

There was a very long pause.

"What's he saying?" Maddy squeaked. She could hardly stand the suspense.

"I'm sorry that you don't want to purchase this box, but it's a standard consumer rule—you taste it, you buy it." Henrietta Hudson's voice was polite, but firm.

"*Now* what's he saying?" Maddy's fingernails were pointy enough to cut glass. She scraped them against the side of the stone wall. Snooks' curse tingled back through her fingertips.

"Very good, sir. You've made a reasonable decision. Fifteen dollars, please."

Wow—he did it! Hudson had sold the poison cookies, and at a ridiculous markup. Her little brother was not such a bad Scout after all.

As soon as Maddy saw Hudson trotting back across the street, she dashed after him.

"Nice work, Henrietta!"

"Easy." Her brother dropped the money in her palm. "So you'll do that thing for me? Say, next Monday?"

"Uh-huh."

"And can I keep this tunic?"

"No way." Maddy was still hopeful that the Elf Scouts

would ask her back into the troop. After all, she hadn't meant to bite Quincy; it had been pure instinct after that nasty cat had hissed at her. And she'd barely broken skin, really, it was more of a taste, just enough to scare him. Maddy hadn't meant to also scare the Elves.

"Here's what I don't understand," said Hudson that evening as he and Maddy swung upside down by their knees in the coat closet, an Old World habit that still worked nicely when they needed a stretch. "A cookie can't slay a vampire. I don't get your diabolical scheme, Mads."

Maddy flung out her arms so her knuckles brushed the floor. Her ears were close enough to the ground to hear mice scrabbling under the floorboards. "Think of it as chasing down the wildebeest. When the wildebeest is too tired to move from the poison effects of the dart—or in this case, when Snooks and the Kriks get too sick from the cookies—that's when I move in for the kill."

"Aha. But how? Stakes through their hearts?" asked Hudson. "Silver bullets? Replace their sunblock with vanilla pudding?"

"Just leave the dastardly details to me."

"But here's what I also don't get," said Hudson. "Why would anyone want to chase down a wildebeest?"

Maddy appraised her upside-down brother, wondering if she could trust him. After all, it had been a triumphant day of sibling teamwork. "You wouldn't understand, Crud, but I've got to get to the bottom of the Krik mystery. I think it's my fate."

"Oh, yes. I'm beginning to think a lot about my own

fate, too." Even with his hair standing off his head, Hudson looked as solemn as Maddy had ever seen him. "Like, why did I get to keep my chill nightly transformations? Why am I the only one of us who can communicate with other species?"

Maddy usually would have been irritated to hear Hudson's questions, because they sounded showoff-y. But since he seemed so earnest, so ready to absorb her every word, she confessed, "I think my destiny is not to be a vegan. Let's face it, I'm way more predator than the rest of the family. One drop of blood bug is tastier to me than a crate of perfect apricots. When I'm on the hunt is when I'm at my best. And those Kriks have got my instincts up."

Hudson bit his bottom lip. "Do you honestly think the Kriks are vamps?"

"All I know is pureblood vampires living across the street from hybrids means danger for us, no matter how peaceful they're pretending to be. We need to strike first."

"If you drive them away, Mads, then we inherit their townhouse. That's the Old World rule. Though I'm not sure how it works here." Hudson looked skeptical. "And I don't know why anyone'd want to live in that place."

"Yeah, no kidding. It's almost *too* perfect." Maddy sighed. She couldn't help but sometimes daydream of leading her parents across the street to their new home. Her mother daubing her eyes, her father puffed with pride, her brother and sister trailing behind. A nice change! Lexie always got the lead in school plays and recitals, and she'd won the Presidential Fitness Test three years straight—whereas

Maddy wasn't anything special at drama, and no good at gym on account of her asthma. Then there was Hudson's handsomeness, which got him plenty more attention than he deserved.

It's about time, Maddy decided, that my special talent got noticed.

All she needed to do was smoke out the Kriks. Once they staggered from the safe protection of their home, they'd be easier targets.

Every day, Maddy spied, but the house stayed silent. No bustle of illness, no emergency medical visitors. Nothing. If the von Kriks had been low profile before, they were keeping no profile now. Had the cookies failed her?

"Madison, you're looking a little dried out," her mother mentioned one evening as Maddy slogged past, a filled humidifier tank in each hand. "You and Lexie should switch chores. She's so much stronger than you."

"But I like this chore," panted Maddy.

Her mother reached out and took a grip on one of the humidifiers so suddenly that Maddy lost her balance. "Careful, daughter. Recognize your limits. You might not be as able as you think." Then she took hold of the other humidifier. In her hands, they seemed light as two batons. Mom's warning me, thought Maddy as she watched her mother stride off to set the humidifiers in the hall. She knows I'm up to something, but she can't stop me, either.

By the end of the week, Maddy was in total despair. The cookies hadn't done it. How terrible to feel so fruitlessly fruit bat. Dragging home from school on Friday afternoon,

Maddy

Maddy picked a tick off a poodle and pondered what she'd done wrong. Maybe if she'd diced that garlic, she would have better diffused the fumes . . .

Then she saw it. A square of yellow, fluttering on the von Krik front door. She moved in closer.

The word on the paper said it all: QUARANTINE.

8

DOOMED TO DOOM

Friday night of the Midwinter Social, Pete Stubbe stood outside the Livingstone apartment, checking out Lexie's all-vintage costume—flannel shirt, faded sneakers, and ripped jeans, the classic attire of doomed rock poet Kurt Cobain.

"Grungy," he proclaimed with a nod.

"Thanks." Lexie was happy with the way her costume had turned out. "Swashbuckley," she complimented back. Because Pete was dressed in his favorite dueler's garb—ruffled shirt, long black boots, and the dashing pencil mustache of Zorro. She took the single red rose he offered and tucked it behind her ear. "We sure have 'Dressed for Effect.' Come on in a sec while I do my nightly chore."

"Uh, okay." Pete looked uneasy as he shuffled into the Livingstone living room, where Lexie's parents were rehearsing their new song, "Shiny Cobwebs." "Hi, Mr. and Mrs. Livingstone," he called.

"Hello, Peter," answered Lexie's father in a strained voice. "Lexington, hurry up! You don't want to be late!"

"Yes, go! Go!" agreed her mother.

As pleasant as her parents were to her other friends and neighbors, Lexie was disappointed that they'd never warmed to poor Pete. No matter how nice he was, Pete genuinely upset them. Now Lexie could hear that her father's drumbeats were off as her mother plucked worriedly on her bass guitar. Unfortunately, Lexie had a weirdly similar effect on Mr. and Mrs. Stubbe, who were always trying to shoo Lexie from their home, too. Whenever Pete and Lexie discussed it, they concluded that both of their families not-so-secretly longed for their child to hang out with kids who were more normal than Lexie or Pete.

But Lexie also suspected there might be a bigger reason.

Lexie swung back to the bathroom and scooped a cup of dried wax worms and mealworms from the Bette's Pets feed bag stored behind the toilet tank. She cracked open the bathroom window and spread the worms evenly over the windowsill. Even though they no longer communicated with other winged creatures, the Livingstones long ago had made a pact to offer free meals to them, out of respect to the hardship of foraging.

A pigeon, poised on the outside sill, regarded Lexie in his dime eye. He seemed to want to tell her something. He waddled and twitched in frustration. Her heart tugged. Of the many unexpected sacrifices the Livingstones had made in immigrating to the New World, losing the ability to chat with other animals had pained Lexie most. Only Hudson had retained this gift, and he rarely shared it. He said what went on in the animal kingdom stayed in the animal kingdom.

"Remember to tip the driver, kids," said Lexie's father, swiftly handing over the taxi fare as, over his shoulder, Lexie's mother snapped a quick picture—a sweet if empty gesture, since of course there was no battery in the Livingstone camera.

"Have fun, good-bye," she said with a wave as her father practically pushed Pete out the door.

Fun! Lexie winced from the word. Ever since the night of her non-professed love, Lexie had been avoiding Dylan like the plague. Specifically, the Bombastus Plague of 1837, when the Livingstones and other hybrids, deadly fearful of accidentally siphoning infected blood, had escaped to the one point of the Channel not teeming with bacteria.

For his part, Dylan was as easygoing as ever. He'd even texted Lexie a couple of times this week, asking if she'd hurt herself falling into his garbage can. Lexie could not bring herself to answer. She was through with humiliating herself over Dylan. She would admire him from afar, and that was it.

"No more moping, no more professing, and definitely no more showing off," she told Pete as the taxi pulled up.

"Good plan," he said. "Dylan doesn't deserve you. Hope there's a costume contest. I bet I'll win it. Tonight should be way fun."

That word again.

Inside, the cafeteria had been transformed. Lunch tables had been folded and stacked to give room for a dance floor, and kids bopped to the music and kicked up dozens of pink and silver balloons. Lexie had Mina radared within seconds. Her archrival looked delicately perfect in a lace top and jeans, with a violet ribbon strung through her curls. As soon as their eyes met, Mina pinched Lucy's arm, and the two of them beelined over.

"Dyslexie, ew! Why are you wearing those grimy old pajamas?"

"Oh . . . because . . ." Lexie stared around, trying not to let the confusion appear on her face. Everyone looked great. Nobody had chosen to "Dress for Effect." With the exception of herself and Pete, everyone had Dressed for Style. Compared with Mina, she felt taller and clumsier and more battish than ever.

"And if it isn't Pete Stubbe." Lucy sneered as she eyed Pete's costume. "What's your problem? Did you think this was a Halloween party?"

"Zorro is a romantic figure, appropriate for any social gathering." Pete patted his glue-on mustache.

"Speaking of romantic, you two are perfect for each other." Mina planted her hands on her hips as she stared from Pete to Lexie and back again. "Sometimes I think you two aren't even from the same planet as the rest of us. More like . . . Planet Freak." She shook back her curls as the others hooted. "Ooh, Dylan's here. See ya."

"I never mean to act freakish," said Pete as they watched the girls take off. "And we're dressed just the way we wanted, right?"

" 'I have never failed to fail,' " answered Lexie in a tone she hoped would have made doomed Kurt Cobain proud. Of course, K.C. had been proud to be a freak.

Lexie's eyes followed Mina as she fluttered over to Dylan, who stood with Alex and the rest of their friends in the lunchroom doorway. Kids were grinning and nudging as they noticed Pete's costume. Lexie wished she could share Pete's attitude and not mind if kids didn't totally accept her—except she *did* mind. I had to give up the language of animals, but I don't speak the language of my classmates, either. I don't fit anywhere, thought Lexie.

As if sensing her misery, Pete squeezed her hand. "Let's try some of that strawberry fizz punch."

Fun was nowhere in sight tonight. Sipping artificial strawberry flavor while Pete practiced his fencing moves, Lexie leaned against the wall. Everyone milled around, having a good time. Here Lexie had waited hundreds of years for her first middle school social, and she had read thousands of musty romantic books and poems, and she had spent millions of moments brooding over adorable Dylan, and not one single thing about love had turned out the way she'd thought.

Something pricked her eyes. Lexie blinked. She had read about tears, but never in her hybrid life had she managed to conjure one. Until now. What did it mean? Was it a sign that she was becoming less hybrid and more human?

She caught a teardrop on her finger.

DJ Jekyll's voice boomed. "Okay, Cathedral Middle! Right now, we're inviting everyone to ask your secret crush to one dance. Only your secret crush, though, and one dance only. So get brave, get busy, or get off the dance floor."

Pete tapped her shoulder. "If you think he's worth it, then you better get brave, Lex," he called over the commotion.

"No way." Lexie quickly wiped her tear on her flannel

sleeve. "DJ Jekyll is talking about a *secret* crush. It's no secret I like Dylan."

"It is to me."

Lexie froze. Slowly, she inched around to find Dylan standing right behind her.

"Really?" Lexie was stunned.

Dylan smiled. "Dance with me?"

" 'No one worth possessing / Can be quite possessed.' " At Pete's sudden outburst, Dylan stepped back, palms up.

"Sorry," he said. "I didn't realize." He looked hard at Lexie. "Are you . . . possessed?"

"Not at all," Pete answered for her. "But we came together, and we'll probably leave together, too. You might say Lex and I belong together."

"What are you doing?" Lexie squeaked, pinching Pete's side just as Lucy reeled up and tapped Dylan on the arm.

"Wanna dance, crush?" Lucy giggled. "Mina says I need to be your bodyguard against stalkers." She raised her eyebrows meaningfully at Lexie.

Dylan gave Lexie one last bewildered look. She gazed back at him. Then, his hand caught in Lucy's, he stumbled off. Heart pounding, Lexie watched them go before turning on her friend in frustration.

"Pete," she said, trying to keep her voice calm. "Was that supposed to be chivalrous? I *like* Dylan. You totally messed it up."

Under the blue party lights, Pete's yellow eyes seemed to glitter. Lexie wondered why she hadn't noticed until now that Pete's recent growth spurt meant he'd caught up to her in height. And was that mustache really glue-on? Because it perfectly matched Pete's strange silvery hair. "It might not have been the best timing," Pete admitted as he ladled his fifth cup of punch and downed it in one thirsty sip. "But I was compelled to say it."

"You were compelled to drive away my crush?"

Pete looked dismayed. "When Mina made that remark about us both being from the same planet, something clicked inside me. Like, maybe you and I . . . we . . . ?" He clasped his head in his large, heavy hands. When had Pete's hands become so pawlike? "Or maybe I am the one who's possessed! At nighttime, I can't think as clear as by day. I'm confused, Lex—but I know that's no excuse."

And Pete looked so genuinely embarrassed that Lexie had to forgive him, with a quick touch of her fingers to his cheek. On contact, the tips of her fingers, as well as her ears and her nose, inexplicably tingled. Was it Pete's skin, or hers, that was too hot?

"Let me make it up to you," Pete pleaded. "Time for Plan B."

"What's Plan B?"

"First, we dance. Then, leave it to me."

Lexie nodded. Together, she and Pete swung onto the dance floor. Immediately, Mina joined them, whirling into the group with Alex on her arm. Soon there was no room to move. Everybody had paired up with someone to protect somebody else's crush, Lexie realized. Human behavior was so peculiar.

The music changed, signaling the end of the crush-dance, and Pete bumped deliberately against Lexie so that she jostled Dylan's elbow. His eyes quizzed her.

"Hey, Dylan. Sorry about earlier," Lexie stammered as Pete walked away. "Pete gets protective."

"Sure." Dylan shrugged. "But Pete's not the only problem. You're hard to understand yourself. And you're the first girl I ever met who could spy from a fourth-floor window."

"I wasn't spying, really," said Lexie. "I was planning to profess . . . something."

"Know what I think?" Dylan leaned close toward her ear. "I think you prefer hanging out with freaky Pete Stubbe. I think you like standing on the sidelines with him better than getting to know a normal guy in a normal way."

Lexie was speechless. Was Dylan right? Was freaky Pete doomed to be her destiny? How tragic! Yet Dylan was so boyish, so innocent, so *human*. Maybe she didn't know how to relate to him in a normal way. Maybe she simply wasn't normal enough.

By now, her crush had turned back to his friends. "Watch me," he commanded, and everyone looked over just in time to see Dylan execute one of the world's worst side thrust karate kicks, accompanied by a whoop as he went crashing to the floor.

"Oooof!" Dylan's hands clasped his knee as he rocked back and forth.

"Dancer down!"

"Bring a heating pad!"

"Call an ambulance!"

"Find an ice pack!"

Teachers flew over. Even without her cowbell, Mrs. Mac-Caw took control. "The hospital is only a few blocks. We need a big, strong young man for you to lean on . . ." Her eyes searched for candidates.

"Me." Lexie stepped forward. Another bat stunt, but necessary. After all, she was the strongest person here. She bent down and swept Dylan into her arms.

"Okay, that does it." Mina raised her voice. "Is everyone watching this? Can we all just please admit that this is too weird? That a _regular_ girl does not have the muscle to carry a _full-sized_ guy?"

"But . . . Lexie wins the Presidential Fitness Competition every year," said Alex.

"Yeah, and Mina's always talking against Lex," added Pete in a strong, deep voice. "Remember that time when she said Lex picked her nose with her tongue?"

Everyone nodded. Yes, they remembered. Mina glared at Pete. And now Mrs. MacCaw was leading Dylan and Lexie out of the gym.

"Do you care that I can carry you?" Lexie whispered to Dylan.

"Just don't drop me." Dylan hooked his arms tighter around her neck. Ooh, and he smelled so nice, thought Lexie. Like new sneakers and spearmint gum.

She carried Dylan the whole seven blocks down Lexington Avenue, all the way through the doors of the hospital emergency room. Dylan mustered a smile as Lexie settled him into a wheelchair. "I hope I did break my leg. Then I'll get a cast and everyone can sign it." So cute—even in his pain, Dylan was thinking about his buddies. Lexie gave Dylan a double thumbs-up as he was wheeled off for X rays.

"Goodness, Lexington Livingstone, I'd like to see an X ray of *your* bones," joked Mrs. MacCaw as they settled in the waiting area. "Strong girl. You must drink plenty of milk."

"Mmph." Lexie tried not to gag at the disgusting mental picture of herself drinking milk, which she had not tasted in multiple hundreds of years—except that one time, right after the malted milk shake had been invented.

Her gaze wandered over to a tall, skinny couple standing at the front desk. They looked sick. Not just any kind of sick. Their lips were liverish, their skin lima bean green, their eyes bugged out and glassed over. Lexie was pretty sure she'd seen that illness before. In fact, she was almost certain she'd once had it herself.

"I'm very sorry," the receptionist was telling the sickly couple, "but without your Social Security numbers, you won't be permitted to see a doctor."

"We need help," wheezed the man. "We even quarantined ourselves. We could have pneumonia, or a stomach virus, or yellow fever, or typhus, or dropsy."

"Or worse," coughed the woman. "Much, much worse." Her fingers twisted the black enameled beads of her necklace. Watching, Lexie felt momentarily hypnotized by the necklace's sparkle and glow.

"Even if any of those extremely awful things are true . . ."

The receptionist upturned her hands. "You're not in the computer file. And if you're not on our records, then you don't exist."

"We do exist. We're standing right here."

"I need more proof," said the receptionist. "That's how paperwork works. Our on-call doctor will be out in a few minutes, if you'd like to speak to her."

The couple shuffled off to wait in plastic chairs.

Lexie knew what had to be done. The Argos would want her to risk it. According to the terms of the New World truce, Old Worlders were encouraged to assist fellow Old Worlders. Even if this couple wasn't fruit hybrids, they were definitely newly arrived Old Worlders who had very likely gotten food poisoning off a New World delicacy. Lexie remembered a few years ago becoming quite ill from jelly beans which, as it turned out, were neither made of jelly nor bean, and contained no healthy, natural fruit preserve whatsoever.

Leaving Mrs. MacCaw, Lexie hurried over. "Excuse me. I've seen your symptoms before," she said. "You two have been poisoned. If this hospital can't help you, I can concoct my mother's ancient remedy. Just tell me where you live." Then Lexie uttered some words of the Old World to show that she was a friend.

The couple's expressions changed. Their clammy fingers squeezed Lexie's wrists as they whispered their address in Old World language.

"That's easy," Lexie answered. "You're right in my neighborhood. I'll prepare it tonight, and by tomorrow morning it will be on your doorstep."

"Thank you," croaked the woman.

"Don't thank her yet," gasped the man. "We're still sick."

And then they were gone.

9

AN OLD HOUND KNOWS THESE THINGS

Out of the corner of his eye, Hudson watched his sister tornado over. One minute she was plunked down at the sixth grade's lunch table. Next second, she stood at the head of his.

O Glory Be! O Joyful Tidings! Up until the moment Maddy rapped on the table for attention, Hudson had been worried she'd ditch her end of the bargain.

Kids fidgeted before she'd said a word. Like all the other grades, Mr. Apple's fourth was pretty much incredibly terrified of Maddy.

"Hand over your lunches, brown-baggers," Maddy ordered. "Chop-chop."

One by one, children surrendered their lunches. Only the spitballing lunkhead kid feebly protested. "Why should I?"

"Because," answered Maddy, "you don't want to make me mad, do you?" Her nostrils flared. In the bright lunchroom light, all color drained from her brown eyes, turning them pale as cream, then white, then crystal clear, and then brown again. So quick and so chilling that nobody could say for sure what had just happened. Yet it was enough to send a tingle down every spine, including Hudson's.

Ever since Maddy had confessed that she needed to fulfill her nonvegan destiny, Hudson had noticed his sister embracing her killer instinct. She sucked down the scant winter supply of blood-filled mosquitoes and ticks whenever she could, and as a result her tongue and gums were a deeper, more violent shade of red. Also, Maddy now could move in small tornado bursts, faster than a human eye could follow. These days, she was so speedy that she no longer bothered taking the bus to P.S. 42—but was always there before it pulled up.

Now this trick. Clear eyes. Exclusive to purebloods.

Whenever Hudson thought he should mention Maddy's metamorphosis to their parents, something stopped him. His instinct told him that he and Maddy were in this together. If he was meant to be a Protector, then he needed his sister's Predator help.

The lunk added his lunch to the stack in front of Maddy, who worked so rapidly that Mrs. Westenra, the fifth-grade teacher and today's lunchroom monitor, was not disturbed in her chat with head chef Mr. Lin about his knockout chili-lime salsa. Within minutes, Maddy had unclung every sandwich, sorting food from its wrapping into two sticky piles in front of her. "You see this plastic?" she asked. "Every day I watch you kids carelessly toss it into the regular garbage. I am fed up. Where does it belong?"

Hudson raised his hand. Maddy pointed a bladed finger on him.

"The blue recycling bin?"

"Correct, young Crudson. Kids, you better make friends with the environment. Or else," threatened Maddy, redirecting her finger to accuse the whole group.

"Or else what?" asked Duane.

"Or else! The environment will punish you! It will usher in awful weather! Like ice ages, hailstorms, and droughts. Cannonballs made out of pure stinking pollution will smash down from the sky!" Maddy's speech was causing blue veins to stand up in her neck. "Worst of all," she continued, "I'll be watching you. Even when you're asleep." Then she threw back her head and cackled, long and low.

Hudson frowned. He thought the cannonballs and the cackling were a bit much. Also, Maddy should not have called him Crudson.

"I think you're from my nightmares," whimpered the freckled redhead girl. Which made Hudson feel bad. That girl, whatever her name was, the paper waster, was actually pretty sweet.

"Can we eat now?" asked a kid.

Maddy nodded. Hands slowly reached into the giant sandwich pile, reclaiming their food.

"But if I catch any of you mis-tossing your cling wrap, I will impose a small torture and a hefty fine, and I will write a letter to the Vice President of National Penalties. If you end up rotting in the clink, it's your own wasteful fault. Later, warts." With a parting hiss, Maddy whisked away.

For a moment, the table was spellbound.

The redhead girl broke the ice. Head held high, she walked all the way to the end of the table. As far from Hudson as she could get. A few other kids, after grabbing back their ham-and-cheeses or peanut-butter-and-jellys, did the same.

Soon Hudson and Duane sat alone.

Duane sighed as he swallowed a fish stick. "Sending in your scary sis was a bad call, Hud," he said.

"History has taught us to rule by force, fines, and fear," explained Hudson. "That's how citizens are traditionally protected."

"All I can say is I'm glad I buy hot lunch," answered Duane. "Even when it's rubbery old fish sticks."

Throughout the rest of the week, Hudson the Protector was quietly comforted to see that his class took more time to separate their regular trash from recycling. While these same students weren't very friendly to him, Hudson and Orville agreed in their late-night talks that being a Protector was not a popularity contest. The more Hudson concentrated on beautifying the New World, the more vividly he remembered the Old, when creatures understood recycling—back when there was no word for it. And the more Hudson thought about being a Protector, the stronger his bat-self became. He now could transform for over an hour per night, and as a bat he could fly higher and faster than ever before. Almost at Old World speeds. But Hudson decided to keep these developments to himself.

"Don't know what's gotten into these kids," remarked Mr. Schnur as he watched a fourth-grader scoop gum he wasn't supposed to be chewing from where he'd spit it in the recycling bin, then furtively place it in the regular trash. "I must say it's a pleasant surprise."

"My sister kind of jump-started them into it," Hudson confessed, "with scare tactics."

The janitor rasped a laugh. "Good. Whatever it takes."

It wasn't until later that week that Hudson fully comprehended the sacrifice of Protectorship.

Thursday was Valentine's Day, a day of great joy for P.S. 42. The fourth grade's bank of cubbies was stocked with cards and flowers and cellophane packets containing heart-shaped chocolates or flavored sugar candies.

Hudson prowled over to his cubby. As the handsomest boy in the class, his candy and chocolate haul was always vast and spectacular. So what if he hated candy and regifted it all to Duane? What mattered was that today was his special day, where he was singled out for being exceptionally gorgeous.

Pillowcase in hand, he peered into his cubby. Looked again. Looked harder. Surely there was some mistake. His cubby was dark and empty as a yewn. Whistling, Hudson strutted over to his desk and opened it. He blinked.

Nothing. No flowers. No candy.

Also, some of his eco-flyers had been returned to him.

Then he saw it. Taped inside the desktop, on the back of his eco-tips, a note.

Dear Hudson,
You used to be my special choice,
Now I don't like to hear your voice.
You are my anti-valentine—
It stinks to get a litter fine.
From Your Number One Anti-valentine,
"Freckled Redhead Girl"

Jolted, Hudson crumpled the paper into a ball. He marched to the front of the room to deposit this horrible crime of a valentine into the trash. As he headed back down the aisle, he glowered at the freckled redhead girl. She was meaner than she looked, that heartless redhead girl. She wasn't even paying attention to him. She only had eyes for . . . uh-oh. This was worse than the empty cubby. Worse than an anti-valentine. Hudson could hardly watch, but there was no denying who was burying his nose into the ruffled petals of a pink carnation. That should have been Hudson's carnation.

"Bethany Finn," said Hudson as her name burst unexpectedly through his head. "Why did you give my Valentine's carnation to . . . that lunkhead?"

The lunk looked hurt. "We've been in school together since kindergarten, Hudson. Don't you even know my name?"

Hudson could not answer, because he did not.

"Hudson, get a clue," said Bethany. "Cute isn't everything. You're the pits."

The pits? What did she mean? From the pits of fruits

grew all new delicious fruit, but Hudson had a feeling that Bethany Finn had meant *pit* as in the end-thing you spit out. Because that was just exactly how he felt—spit out of Mr. Apple's fourth grade.

Spit out and heading home at the end of the lonely day, Hudson ran into his mother's dog pack. The half dozen small dogs (his father exercised the larger breeds) were tied to a bike stand outside a Park Avenue apartment building. Hudson whistled hello. Dogs barked greetings.

At least not everyone was shunning him.

Sherlock was an old basset hound whom Hudson's mother had been walking for years. He was the first pure animal who had befriended Hudson in the New World. This afternoon, as always, slobber dribbled in strings from his jowls. Hudson crouched and used his shirtsleeve to wipe it up.

"How's it going, Sherlock?"

"Looking forward to warmer months and packing away this ugly dog sweater." Sherlock snuffled. "Give a dog a scratch between the shoulders?"

Hudson scratched. "Where's Mom?"

"She's dropping off Scrumptilicious," yapped Daisy, the one-eyed pug.

"Fifty-fourth floor," yipped Chico, a terrier mix. "They're probably still in the elevator. Me, I don't care for views. I'm more of a burrower." He demonstrated, clawing into the pavement. Then he spied his tail and started chasing it.

"Who's Scrumptilicious?" asked Hudson.

"Toy poodle." Sherlock yawned, creating fresh chains of slobber.

"Did you check out those pink booties Scrump was wearing?" panted Chico, and then he did a flouncy impression. The dogs barked with laughter. Myrtle the corgi laughed so hard, she fell over.

"Watch it, Myrtle," said Sherlock, nosing her back onto her feet. "You might look perky, but you're ninety-one in dog years."

"Eighty-four," snapped Myrtle.

"Why the long face?" Sherlock asked Hudson.

"School," Hudson answered. "Sometimes my differences take up more space than my sameness."

"Yeah, we know what that's like," said Sherlock.

"You?" Hudson stared around the pack. "How?"

"Rrrf, think about it. It's no picnic walking in one dog pack of seven different breeds," explained Sherlock. "For example, Bernie's legs are too short, which slows us all down."

"Aw, gimme a break," said Bernie, who was a dachshund and very self-conscious about his legs. "They get the job done."

"And Myrtle's getting long in the tooth, and Daisy's missing an eye, and Chico's a drama queen, and now we've got Scrumptilicious," continued Sherlock, "with her silly name and pink booties. Scrump really lowered our coolness quota."

"And you, Sherlock? It's not like you're some kinda Best

in Show." Bernie snorted. "Your saliva issues mean a rainy-day forecast *every* day for the rest of us."

Sherlock shook off the insult, sending slobber everywhere. "That's exactly my point. Admit your differences, and people forgive. A little goodwill goes a long way."

Hudson prickled. Admitting was practically the same as apologizing, and apologies made him feel dumb, and he never liked to feel dumb. What if he admit-apologized to the class, and everyone laughed at him? What if they didn't accept his apology? What if they didn't give him the Protector respect he deserved? "How do you know if that'll work?"

"Trust me," said Sherlock. "An old hound knows these things."

The next day was Friday. All of Mr. Apple's students' memoir projects were put up around the room for display. Hudson had assembled his own project with scant enthusiasm. His was the most boring because he hadn't been able to use his real Old World history or take any photographs. Next to his blah, phony essay, he'd brought in his completed, thawed-out Caspian Sea jigsaw puzzle. Lastly, he had painted a watercolor of his family as seen from an aerial view so they were just little specks.

Hudson didn't expect to get a good grade on this project, but in a fruit-vampire-bat hybrid family, it was way more important not to call attention to heritage.

The girl with the white eyebrows who was from Sweden had brought in a blender and showed the class how to make lingonberry juice. Hudson drank a whole cup and repeated her name so that he was sure he remembered it before he said, "I really like your project, Vendela Sorkin."

"Oh, um, thanks, Hudson." Vendela Sorkin took a cautious step away from him. "And tell your sister I'm bringing my lunch in earth-friendly reusable containers now, okay?"

Hudson nodded. He didn't even unplug Vendela's blender to save energy, though his fingers itched to. Instead, he slowly made his way around the room, praising the projects. It was hard work, and gradually he realized that one nice word for each project was not enough to win the class's forgiveness.

One kid, passing by Hudson's project, whispered very loud, "I vote Hudson's memoir most recyclable."

"Shh," warned the other kid, "or he'll send his thug sister to beat you up."

Hudson, hearing this, suddenly experienced a terrible burning in his face. He thought this must be blushing—his first blush, ever. His fingers pressed his flaming cheeks. Did this shameful feeling mean he was becoming more human?

At the end of the day, with Mr. Apple's permission, Hudson gathered his courage and stood before his fellow students. "Class, my message to help balance our ecosystem had too much clout. While this message is still critical, I want to make a goodwill offering. Therefore, everyone is invited to a party at my home on the last day of this month. It is my parents' anniversary and usually we just like it to be family. So consider yourselves lucky. Please bring fruit and leave by dinnertime. Thank you." Now Hudson pulled a box of Elf Scout cookies from his knapsack. "Help yourself to these. I forgot to give gifts for Valentine's Day. Better late than never." He opened the box and set it on Mr. Apple's desk.

The class didn't speak. Hudson wondered why they all looked so frightened.

"Count me in, Hudson," Mr. Apple said at last, breaking the silence. He clapped one hand on Hudson's shoulder as he used the other to select a cookie. "I, for one, would like to get to know you better by visiting your home. Sometimes a family doesn't bloom to life out of a simple class project. We can do it all as a field trip, with permission notes from parents. Right, kids?"

The class spoke not a word. Not one peep. Nobody went for a buttercrumbly, either. Mr. Apple's extra-cheerful crunching was the loudest noise in the classroom.

Hudson slunk to his desk. Every pore of his paper-thin vampire skin felt dry and thirsty and exhausted. He had complimented and admitted and even—*shudder*—apologized, and he probably hadn't solved anything at all.

In fact, he was sure of it.

10

TEA FOR YOU

"Idiot! You blithering idiot!" Maddy flew from one end of the family room to the other. As soon as she hit the wall, she jump-kicked it, using her boot as a lever to somersault midair to land and pounce to the other end. It was making her dizzy, but had the benefit of upsetting her sister. "Why did you prepare those icky von Kriks an Old World healing brew and put in on their doorstep, Hex? After all my hard work, you wrecked everything!" Swoosh, whoosh, kick, flip, swoosh.

Hudson looked up from his latest jigsaw puzzle of Gangehi Island. "Cut it out. You're scuffing the wall."

Maddy was not ready to cut it out.

"How was I supposed to know you'd deliberately poisoned our neighbors?" asked her sister, looking up from her toenails, to which she was adding a second coat of *rouge noir*. "I didn't realize they were your precious von Kriks. They looked like hybrids that'd gotten indigestion off some too-human food, like mayonnaise or licorice logs. So I got out the Old World *Healing Balms* book and made a poultice."

"Which one?" asked Hudson.

"The same detoxifier Mom gave me when I ate those

jelly beans. When you crush burnt matchsticks with five goose feathers and water from a moonlit puddle."

Hudson nodded. "Mom made gallons of it during that last Old World War, too, when some fruits ate beef jerky that they thought was dried fig."

A mosquito was poised on the wall. Midsomersault, Maddy's cherry-red tongue shot out. She landed on both feet and crunched.

Lexie shuddered. Maddy bared her fangs. Lexie hid her eyes. "Don't show me your teeth when they're bloody."

Maddy bared them some more.

"You know, Mads, you're getting scarier." Lexie turned to Hudson. "The other day she made her eyes go clear."

"You shouldn't tattle," reprimanded Hudson. He exchanged a significant look with Maddy. Good ol' Crud, he was smart to be on her side.

"Clear eyes means there's too much blood in your diet." Lexie wagged her finger. "I better report to Mom and Dad. I don't care if it's tattling."

"They'd agree I need the extra protein." Maddy spat a crunchy ball of bug wings and legs, then did another flip.

"Hey!" Now her sister peered forward. "When did you get your ears pierced!?"

"Last week. They're silver studs. I was planning to fire them out of Hudson's air pellet gun straight into the von Kriks—before you went and cured them."

"Please. That's a toy gun." Hudson sighed. "Its pressure wouldn't hurt a chipmunk. What do you think the undead are made of, Maddy? Cheese soufflé?"

Maddy

"It would have worked if they'd stayed cookie-poisoned," Maddy insisted.

Lexie's expression challenged her. "Slurp down all the bugs you want, but you're too fruit-mix, Maddy. All you're going to do is get in more trouble than you know how to get out of. You've got to learn how to ignore the Kriks."

Easy for fruity Lexie to say. Maddy clenched her fists. It was horrible to feel so vampirey without enough power to do anything about it. If she were a true pureblood, the Kriks might have befriended her. As an enemy hybrid, all she could do was pester them and hope they moved away. But ignore the Kriks? Never. Their daily presence was nothing but an agitation. She turned a final somersault, then slumped onto the window seat. She didn't even want to spy. Spying was for fruits.

Lexie hopped off to the kitchen and soon returned with a platter of apples, strawberries, tomatoes, and carrots fanned out just the way dishes were presented at Candlewick. "As the oldest, I demand you eat everything on this plate," she said. "I even brought you a glass of cold water to help it go down."

"Gross!" Maddy pushed the plate away. "No, thanks."

"If you don't eat this fruit, I'll tell Mom and Dad who made those scuff marks, and who got her ears pierced without permission."

"That's called blackmail."

"Actually, it's called the truth."

Something in her older sister's face made Maddy

take the plate. "Fine. I'll eat it, but only because you're so annoying."

She'd just washed down her last slice of apple when the telephone rang. They all looked around in wonder. The phone never rang. Since everyone used cell phones, nobody even knew exactly where the telephone was located.

Brrr-rrrring! Now Livingstones went scrambling.

"It's in the games closet!"

"It's behind the bookshelf!"

Maddy's ears were best. She rolled under the couch and picked up. "What?"

"Is that any way to say hello?" asked the sugary voice on the other end of the line.

"Who is this?" But Maddy knew. Her blood surged.

"We are inviting you over for tea, neighbor."

"Really?" As excited as she was, Maddy tried to sound casual. "Why are you being so nice to me?"

"We think you've had a misimpression of us, Maddy." Nicola's voice tinkled sweetly. "We want to clear things up. Come over to the window and wave hello."

So Maddy crawled out from under the couch and used her spyglasses to look through the window. At the pay phone across the street, Nicola von Krik, in a big floppy hat and buttoned-up trenchcoat, stood smiling and waving.

"What's ol' Nic von Krik up to now?" whispered Hudson.

Maddy put her hand on the receiver. "She's inviting me over for tea."

"You should go," said Lexie. "That way, you can face-to-face apologize for the trouble you've been causing them."

Maddy nodded. "Give me two minutes," she said into the phone. She clicked off and smirked. "Good point, Lex. Making up with the von Kriks will win their trust. Then I'll take them by surprise when I shine Dad's solar-power flashlight on them. If they're real purebloods, their skin will shrivel."

At that, Hudson's face clouded over. "Wait! Something fishy is going on with that invitation. And what do you think two angry purebloods are capable of, if they gang up together against one hybrid?" he asked sternly. "Who do you suppose would win that one?"

Now Lexie looked fearful. "Maybe you shouldn't go, Maddy. You've taken this too far."

"Oh, stop worrying. Later, bunions." Maddy adopted an air of ease as she pulled on her coat and sunglasses, then tucked her inhaler, flashlight, and notepad into her pocket.

Hudson caught up to her at the front door. "I'll stay in the family room. So if you need to echolocate, you know where to bounce an S.O.S." He looked grave. "If you need me," he whispered, "I'll be right over. I'll protect you."

"Yeah, yeah." Although Maddy was quietly relieved to hear her brother's courageous words. Crudson was turning out to be not so cruddy, after all.

She made herself think all-brave thoughts as she approached the unfriendly lion door knockers. She decided on the doorbell instead.

Snooks appeared with a smooth bow and crooked grin. "Welcome, invited guest." As the word "invited" left his lips, the servant's curse blew off as soft as a puff on a summer dandelion. Maddy strolled easily through the front door.

"The Master is napping. Madam is indoor sledding," informed Snooks. "I'm accompanying her with this cheerful piece of music called 'Moonlight Sonata.'" He moved off to the grand piano and began to play. Beautiful music filled air.

"Darling, look up . . ."

And Maddy looked up.

At the top of the stairs, Nicola was kneeling on a heavy silver serving tray. "Wheeeeeeee!" she squealed, pushing off. Maddy watched in fascination as Nicola first bounced, then skimmed down the stairs headfirst at an alarming bobsleigh speed, leaning into the curve of the banister, all the way to the bottom where, with a final whoosh, she shot past the first step, catching air, and then—

Bang! Both Krik and tray hit the floor and skidded across to stop at Maddy's boots.

"Oh, exquisite fun! I rate myself a nine point six!" Nicola applauded herself. Then she stood and brushed off and picked up the tray, racing all the way back up the steps. She rubbed it down with a soft cloth. "Shined for speed. Your turn, Maddy. I dare you."

Maddy hesitated. Obviously, it wasn't the speed that bothered her. It just seemed like such a long, steep, twisty ride from top to bottom. She couldn't rely on Hudson's wings or Lexie's strength, only her own sneakiness, which didn't count for much in speed-and-strength moments.

But a dare was a dare. Maddy drew a breath and galloped up to meet Nicola on the landing.

"Hold tight to the handles," said Nicola as Maddy kneeled on the tray, hunkering down. "That's the trick." Then two strong hands pushed her off.

"Eeeeeeeeeee!" A burst of speed, the carpeted steps rumpity-bumpiting under her, the flashlight flying out of her pocket in another direction, a final bump, then, swoosh, airborne—smack!—the platter touched bottom, and now she was gliding breathless to a graceful stop at the front door.

"I did it!" Maddy laughed. "I rate myself a nine point seven." She tried to applaud herself but her hands held their grip. She tugged. "My fingers are stuck to the tray." She wriggled. "My knees, too, and my cloak—ew, there's sticky all over me." Suddenly she realized. "Hey! I'm glued! I'm glued!"

At the top of the landing, Nicola laughed menacingly. "As I said, that's the trick!"

"You didn't rub down this tray for speed," said Maddy as a cold pit fell in her stomach. "You put super-sticky glue all over it."

"*Extra*-super-sticky glue! And I rate you a silly munchkin!" Nicola cackled again. Maddy recognized that imitation. Count Chocula.

Snooks continued pounding on the piano. In Maddy's ears, this music didn't sound cheerful, but extraordinarily melancholy. Suddenly Maddy recalled when she'd gotten lost from her family during an Old World outdoor Oktoberfest. It had been impossible to echolocate anyone while all the oompah music played. The live band had completely scrambled the radar. As it was doing now.

"Crud! Crud!" She wriggled helplessly on her tray as she bounced her brother's name into the music static. "Hudson! Help help help!"

"Help help help!" Nicola imitated as she skipped downstairs and hoisted the weighted tray, with Maddy on it, so that both were held aloft over her head.

"Final proof," Maddy gasped. "You *do* pick up echo wave frequency, and you're as strong as—"

"A pureblood vampire," finished Nicola calmly. "Which is exactly what I am." The tray swayed as Nicola crossed the marble floor. No matter how hard Maddy pitched left or squirmed right, Nicola did not once lose balance. It was as if her skeleton were made out of steel. Maddy suddenly felt very, very small, and very, very stuck.

"Then why are you here?" she asked. "I thought purebloods preferred the Old World."

"A lot of vampires are renouncing eternity and moving to Manhattan. There's just so much to do here," said Nicola. "Like getting seaweed wrap massages and ordering all this delicious human food such as Chinese takeout—which I'm sure tastes a lot better than you, Maddy. Especially since you're a fruit-hybrid, it's very likely that you'll be much too sour."

"You don't *have* to taste me," Maddy mentioned.

"Of course we do, silly. You are simply the most awful creature Nigel and I have ever encountered." By now, they had entered the dining room.

"The Argos will catch you," Maddy cautioned. "Slaying me violates the New World truce. You'd be exiled before the next sunrise."

Nicola sighed. "Do you think we're stupid? We've already made arrangements to freight-ship ourselves to an undisclosed location aboard a Fiesta Cruise ship. After we have you for tea, that is, you dumb little girl."

"Well, I'm not so dumb that you didn't escape my poison buttercrumb . . ." Maddy's voice trailed off when she saw that the dining room table was already set for two. A cozy fire crackled in the fireplace, candles burned low in the candelabras, and all the vases were filled with thorny bloodred roses.

"Tea is served," sang Nicola as she positioned the tray full of Maddy between the two place settings. "Come out, come out."

"Come out, come out who? From where?" Maddy squeaked.

"If you'd added more chunks of raw garlic, you might have actually slain us, Maddy." Nigel's voice was soft. "That cookie trick was much too cruel for a part-fruit. But in the end, not cruel enough. We're lucky your big sister is so kind, eh?"

Maddy stared around. "Where are you, Nigel?"

From under the table came the sound of a heavy lid

being lifted and scraped back. Then Nigel appeared, looking sleepy but elegant in a dark running suit.

"Crud is *finally* wrong about something." Maddy sighed. "Those weren't clothes trunks, after all. Coffins, one hundred percent." Her relief that Hudson could be wrong sometimes was marred knowing that von Kriks would soon be feasting on her blood.

"Time for Maddy tartar." Nigel rubbed his spindly hands together. "Sorry, Maddy. Better luck next life." He snapped open his linen napkin and tucked it into his collar. "Dearest Nicola, you must take the first bite of her."

"No, darling, I insist, you first."

"You."

"No, you."

"How about both of you go together?" suggested Maddy. "If this is my grim destiny, let's get it over and done with."

"Good idea," said the von Kriks in unison.

Maddy sat up straight and closed her eyes. Disappointed as she was to be so heartlessly tricked, she knew that an expert vampire bite was not nearly as painful as falling off the top of a building or being struck by lightning—both of which had happened to her, and had taken quite a while to recover from.

Each Krik leaned forward and sunk fangs into her neck. A tingling filled Maddy's body. It was as if her veins were being filled with dense liquid that was making her strong and powerful. Was she devoured yet? Because, really, it wasn't at all bad. So nice that at first Maddy didn't notice the humming in her ears.

"Mmmmmm! Mmmmmm!"

"Arright, I'm sure I taste great. You don't have to rub it in," muttered Maddy.

"Mmmmm! Mmmmmm!"

Maddy opened her eyes. A whorl of fur, a whir of wings, a flash of dark, dancing eyes—hey, she knew that bat! But how had Hudson managed to transform by day?

Both von Kriks had detached from her and were now ducking and reeling around the room to avoid a Hudson-the-bat attack. But something else was wrong with them. Why were they clutching at their throats? Why were they gargling and choking?

Nigel staggered backward and crooked a finger on her.

"You got us—again!" he wheezed, and then his finger fell off, dropping from his hand like a stick of chalk and breaking apart like a grotesque buttercrumbly as it landed on the carpet.

Maddy gaped. As he'd spoken, Nigel's face, wan and waxen, had cracked like a china cup into a thousand pieces. She turned to see a duplicate horror as a brittle and splintering Nicola dropped into a chair.

"Your blood . . . too sweet . . . ," cawed Nicola faintly, and then, before Maddy's disbelieving eyes, she collapsed. Joint by joint, tiny flakes of Nicola broke off and crumbled to fine powder. All that was left was a pile of dust, upon which rested her glittering black beaded necklace. With a groan and a soft *phuff*, Nigel dropped next, as if a trapdoor had opened beneath his feet.

By this time, Hudson had flown from the room, and the music had stopped. Snooks appeared in the door. "Suppose I ought to find a broom and dustpan."

"How'd I do that?" Maddy inched her tray forward for a better look at the soft mound of hair, clothes, dust, and linen napkins that had once been von Kriks.

"Not sure, but . . ." Snooks dropped to kneel before her. "I am now at your service, little shrimp. And I hope you'll give me more time off for holidays than those cheap Kriks."

"No problem," said Maddy. "But if that's really the way the cookie crumbles, then you can start by figuring out how to unstick me from this tray and handing me that black bead necklace. Chop-chop."

11

TRICK OF THE MOON

Lexie was honestly shocked. "You mean the thermos was full of holy water?" She wrinkled her nose. "I only used it because I found it in the fridge and it was cold."

"Looks like that water you gave Maddy helped to save her life." Hudson stretched his bony arms to touch the lip of the cracked porcelain tub. The three Livingstone kids were all hanging upside down and side by side from the shower rod in one of the many moldy bathrooms of the old von Krik house.

"It wasn't all me. You were brave, sis," said Lexie generously. "You probably thought you were done for. You must have felt so alone."

"Oh, I had some extra help," said Maddy with a secret smile at Hudson. "Anyway, all's well that ends well, since the Argos gave us the deed to this perfectly fantastic townhouse."

"Mmm," Lexie answered.

Their parents had explained to Lexie and Hudson that Maddy saw the von Krik house differently from the rest of them. "There are some vampires who can see deeper into the past, at how things used to look. Instead of the way they are today," their father had explained. Which meant what Maddy viewed as a stunningly beautiful townhouse, the other Livingstones saw for what it really was—a dark, dank, leaky, creaky, dreary old hunk of stone.

Lexie wasn't sure she'd ever feel comfortable in it, but rules were rules. The battered parcel that came in the mail last week from the Old World had not only contained Maddy's ruby-and-gold-dagger slayer's pin but also the official transfer deed of the von Krik property to the Livingstones.

"I'm glad the Argos and the Old World ruled that your double-slay was self-defense," their mother had said, pinning the pin on a proud Maddy. "And I have to admit, I do like being a home owner better than renting. Though you'll never stop worrying me, Madison."

Lexie left it to her parents to admire Maddy's courage, but her own fruit blood curdled in apprehension. The von Krik victory had made Maddy brave, and a tiny bit of their puncture-wound blood now coursed through her. Lexie worried that it wouldn't be long before her sister targeted her next victim.

Meanwhile, moving—even moving across the street—meant lots of work, especially since the Livingstone parents had decided to send Snooks away on a monthlong Fiesta Cruise. When they weren't scrubbing at rot and fungus, or mopping the dust-carpeted floors, the kids were hang-and-stretch testing all the coat racks and the closet, shower, and curtain rods. It was a solid house with lots of nooks for hiding and swooping and roosting. And no amount of scrub and polish could get rid of the smell, not even for the special occasion of their parents' three hundred ninety-fifth wedding anniversary, which was now also a house-warming party and their first-ever big celebration in the New World.

The smell of the Old World, mused Lexie as she walked inside, back from yet another errand to the Candlewick Café. Like the coffins we used to sleep in. Wet wood and mildew and stale ale. And ghosts, too. Though she hadn't met one yet, she could smell them creeping around, quiet as cockroaches, waiting for the right opportunity to reveal themselves.

" 'The Spirits of the dead, who stood In Life before thee, are again, In death, around thee,' " Lexie quoted out loud, hoping to conjure a couple as she joined her mother, who was in the kitchen scooping cantaloupe and honeydew melon balls for her signature seven-fruit salad.

"Careful," said her mother, taking the Candlewick bags. "We've got enough company coming without needing to raise up a bunch of ghosts."

"Speaking of company, now that we've got all this room, I say we invite some pigeons to live in the attic," Lexie suggested. "And maybe some nice mice, too?"

Her mother shook her head no. "Stray critters are too tempting for your sister. We have to keep watch on her appetite. Too much protein in Maddy's diet isn't safe."

"Mom, why is Maddy so lethal? It doesn't make sense." Lexie shook her head over the question that had been stuck in it all week. "Sometimes it's hard to believe she's my full-blood sister."

Her mother said nothing, but was scooping melon balls double-time. When Lexie glanced at her out of the side cracks of her eyes, her mother looked tense.

"Your sister, Madison," she began softly, "is not—" And then the doorbell rang. "Our first guests!" Her mother dropped the melon scooper and patted her hair. "How do I look?"

"Great." Although ever since Hudson had requested that the family please cut down using the dry cleaner's on account of their environmentally damaging chemicals, their father had taken on the chore of ironing the family clothes. As a result, the laundry was either scorched or wrinkly. Today, her mother's shirt was little bit of both. But Lexie didn't have the heart to say anything.

"I hope everyone likes fruit and veggies and soy." Her mother looked at the decorative platters of vegan food, some homemade and some from Candlewick.

"Of course they will. I'll get the door." Lexie took off the apron that protected her new dress. She had found it in her favorite thrift shop. The lace scratched, but she thought it looked unfreakish and undoomed and party-perfect.

"Mr. Apple!" Lexie smiled as she opened the creaky front door. "Come on in."

Her former fourth-grade teacher beamed. "Look at you, Lexie. All grown up." Behind Mr. Apple was Hudson's entire class. Each child was holding an item of fruit. None of them looked happy to be there.

"Holy trick-or-treat, is this a real-live Halloween house or what?" hissed one of kids.

103

"Haunted," whispered another. "Definitely haunted."

A redheaded girl thrust a cantaloupe into Lexie's arms. "We heard that if we didn't come, Hudson's *other* sister would eat our eyeballs with a knife and fork and salt and pepper."

"Or skin us alive," piped up another fourth-grader.

"Or chop off our toes and feed them to ducks," whispered another.

"Now, where would you get a silly idea like that?" Lexie shook her head. "Maddy would never do such terrible things. Follow me, and I'll show you why you have nothing to worry about."

The class dragged in. "See?" Lexie pointed out her sister, who sat at the piano, smiling and playing "Moonlight Sonata" and looking very lovely, Lexie decided, in her robin's egg blue uniform and new black glass bead necklace. Too bad she had blown it with the real Elf Scouts. Now Lexie crossed her fingers to protect herself from the white lie she needed to tell to set all fourth-grade minds at ease. "Maddy's an Elf Scout. That means she made an official vow to be thoughtful, helpful, and kind."

There was some conferring among the others. *"I never saw an Elf Scout pin that was shaped like a knife." "She's still got those mean, pointy teeth!" "But what're those Band-Aids on her neck for?"*

Lexie pretended not to hear them. "So you don't have to be scared of Maddy," she said brightly.

Nobody looked too sure about that.

The doorbell continued to ring. Every time, Lexie answered it expectantly, but the person on the other side of the door was never Dylan. Would he show up at all?

Big Bill from Candlewick came, as did other members of her parents' band, the Dead Ringers, and lots of their Wander Wag dog-walking clients with their dogs. But no Dylan. At least the fourth-graders seemed more at ease once the dogs arrived. Soon the party got noisy.

Maybe Dylan's never coming, thought Lexie. Her mind filled like floodwater with poems about waiting, yearning, aging, dying, and not meeting up with your one true love until the crucial minute right before you drank poison or got stabbed in the heart.

Then Pete arrived, dressed as Alexander Hamilton, his second-favorite dueler. "Pete!" Lexie couldn't believe her eyes. "You look so . . ." Handsome, she had been about to say. Then she felt too shy. Pete seemed taller, maybe—much taller now than Lexie. And broader across the shoulders. But there was something else. Something she could not quite put her finger on.

"I might have to leave soon," said Pete. "As in, as soon as it gets dark." He plucked at his cravat. He looked nervous. A gloss of sweat shone along his hairline.

"Sure." Lexie shrugged. Pete could get worked up about strange things. Like the dogs, which were snuffling and yapping. They seemed to have taken an unusual interest in Pete.

The doorbell rang again. Dylan, at last. Lexie breathed a sigh of relief. He was propped on crutches to balance the weight of his fiberglass cast. On his one side was Mina.

On the other was Lucy. Surrounding them were Alex, J.C., Keely, Fred, and Davina—the whole gang.

"Hope you don't mind the extra crew," said Dylan. "I didn't invite them, but they came anyway."

"We always go where Dylan goes," said Mina with a laugh.

"Right." Lexie's voice was small. "Come in. Beverages are in the dining room."

"I really like your granny dress, Lex," said Lucy with a sniff. "Did it come free with bifocals and a cane?"

"Raise your hand if you're surprised that Lexie lives in the scariest house in New York City," Mina added as they all trooped inside. "Dylan, you sit there. I'll be back with some snacks. If they're not too gross and freaky."

"And if it isn't Pete Stubbe, all dressed up to look like a—" but then Lucy stopped and looked the suddenly improved Pete up and down. "Pete . . . um . . . you want to show me the buffet?"

Pete shrugged, but Lexie could tell he was pleased with Lucy's attention as they went off together.

"So, L.L., gonna sign my cast?" Dylan flashed his perfect smile as he settled back on one of the sagging loveseats and leaned his crutches against the faded wallpaper. "I even got this special green pen." He pulled it out from behind his ear.

Lexie sat next to Dylan and uncapped the pen. She stared at Dylan's cast. So many people had signed it that the cast was colored more green than white. She started to write one place, then another. Then she gave up. "Dylan, there's no room for my name," she said, trying and failing to keep the tremor out of her voice. She felt so incredibly unspecial. Just another name on Dylan's crowded cast.

"Yes, there is, see? Right up here." Dylan leaned forward and tapped the place between two wriggling toes. "For your entire name. All six syllables."

For a while, Lexie stared at the slip of space reserved just for her. Dylan had so many friends, it was daunting. There was no way she could make that scrap of space special unless . . . Quickly, while Dylan wasn't looking, Lexie bit her finger deep enough so that she broke skin. A drop of dry blue-green blood welled up on the tip of her finger. She pressed the point of Dylan's pen into the blood, then bent forward and signed her name in her very best Old World calligraphy.

Lexyngton Livyngsfone

"Nice!" Dylan whistled when he saw her handiwork. Then he looked closer. "Hey, all the letters are kinda raised up, and the ink's a different green. That's amazing, Lex. How'd you do that?"

Lexie smiled and shrugged. A mix of blood and ink was the standard signature for Old World vampire hybrids, but Dylan didn't need to know that. Now, for as long as Dylan wore this cast, he would see her name first. "It *is* a funny color. Your pen must be running out of ink or something."

"Yeah, really amazing," Mina had appeared with a plate

of tofu crab cakes in hand. "Like your rotating legs and how you can carry a grown boy seven blocks, or any of the other abnormal things about you. I saw you bite your finger, Lexie. What are you made out of, anyway? Martian goop?" All at once, Mina reached forward and pinched Lexie's arm, hard.

"Yowch!" Lexie stared in shock at the mark Mina had made.

"Look at her skin, everyone!" Mina pointed. "It's not pinchy-pink! It's beasty-bluey-green!"

"Because I'm anemic," said Lexie, rubbing the blue-green pinch spot. "It means I'm low on iron. Which makes my blood funny."

"Whatever," Mina scoffed. "Let's see the giant bite mark on your finger."

Lexie showed her finger. By now, the wound had halfway healed. In Old World days it would have been completely gone. Still, it was proof enough.

"See, Mina. Lexie didn't bite herself," Dylan said exasperatedly. "And everyone knows she's on a special fruit diet. Don't make her feel all self-conscious about her blood." Coming from cool Dylan, the other kids easily accepted this logic. Mina simmered.

"Something's up with you, Lex," she fumed. "Something really odd, and one day, I'll get to the bottom of it. You can count on that."

Before Lexie could answer, she felt a tap on her shoulder, then a whisper in her ear. "I'm heading out." She turned. It was Pete, looking more nervous and more intensely handsome even than when she'd seen him just minutes ago.

"What's wrong?" As soon as Lexie stood, Mina plopped herself right down in the space on the loveseat next to Dylan.

"It's getting dark."

"So? Call your parents. Or stay over. We've got so many rooms now. My parents won't mind." Lexie laughed. "What are you, scared of the dark?"

"Kind of." There was an urgency in Pete's voice that Lexie hadn't heard before.

"Okay, okay." As she showed him out to the door, Lexie noticed that Pete's hair looked thicker, coarser, more silvery. Also, the fabric of his frock coat was beginning to pull against his broad, weightlifter's back. But since when did Pete have a broad, weightlifter's back?

Lexie's fruit instincts went into high alert. Something inhuman was happening to her friend.

When she creaked open the door, Pete winced. He stepped squinting out into the night as if it were noonday on the sunniest beach.

"Pete, is there something you want to tell me?" Lexie asked him.

"Nothing you don't know already," he growled. By a trick or the brightness of the full moon, he appeared to have sprouted yet another inch. How did he look so familiar, yet so newly magnificent? Her brain was on overload, yet her thoughts seemed scrambled, like shooting stars. Before she knew what she was doing, Lexie leaned up and kissed the prickly stubble of Pete's cheek.

"See you at school, Lex." Pete's voice was pure gravel. He reached his hand to touch the place her kiss had landed. Their eyes locked, then Pete loped off into the night.

In the distance, Lexie heard a faint sound. It was Pete, howling.

And in that second Lexie knew. Pete was no mere freak. By the light of the moon, she knew the truth that perhaps she'd always suspected. Why her parents had not warmed to Pete, and why the Stubbes weren't always glad to see Lexie. Her quirky pal was one of the rarest of creatures. Pete Stubbe was a werewolf.

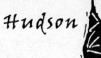

12

MILES TO GO

It was sort of fun being a host, Hudson thought, as he continued to circle the party. "Hello, Elliot Pierce. Hi, Marcus MacCorkle. What's up, Jasmine Danielle?" With help from Mr. Apple, Hudson had memorized each fourth-grader's name. Even the lunk, who officially went by the name Charlie Easterby. "Hi there, Charlie Easterby."

Unfortunately, the chunky lunk was so scared of Maddy that his teeth couldn't stop chattering long enough to return Hudson's greeting. So Hudson also made sure every single kid met his other, nicer sister, Lexie.

Hudson had been watching Lexie's friend Pete Stubbe all night. As a fellow night creature, he had noticed immediately that Pete was transforming. Then, when Pete asked Hudson where the bathroom was, he accidentally spoke in a dog dialect.

"There's a private one up the stairs, first door on the left," Hudson told Pete. As Pete bounded up the stairs, using his arms to give himself extra speed, Hudson noticed an older man watching him. He had seen him earlier, mingling quietly among the partygoers. As Pete bounded back down the stairs, the old man gave Hudson a meaningful look, then moved off. Something in his thoughtful black eyes nudged at Hudson's memory. Why was the old man so familiar?

Slowly, as the moon came out and Hudson's night vision spiked and his night thoughts shone clear, he began to understand.

The old man was also Orville.

The old man was the school janitor, Mr. Schnur.

The old man was also an Argos.

Nobody else seemed to notice the man as he moved soundlessly across the room. But Hudson watched him. When he brushed against Dylan Easterby's cast, the raised Old World signature that Lexie had spontaneously scribbled immediately changed back to flat, uninteresting green cursive. When he walked toward the pantry, his finger ran along the wall and instantly erased all of the scuff marks Maddy had made during yesterday's marathon backflip session. Hudson had always believed in a stern and punishing Argos, but this man worked with such gentle care. Were all the Argos like that?

Lexie had rushed back into the party wild-eyed after showing Pete the door. Not a moment too soon, thought Hudson. Poor old Pete was about to start howling any second.

"Did you finally see a ghost?" he asked innocently, plucking a blueberry off a fruit shish kabob. "I think there's one who haunts the library."

"Almost." Lexie's face was bright with excitement. "Hudson, have you ever known somebody for a really long time, and you thought you knew everything about them, but as it turned out, the most important thing about them was kept a complete secret from you?"

"Is this about Pete being a hybrid?" he asked.

His sister's eyes widened. "How did you know?"

"Animals know who the other animals are. I think he's some kind of dog."

"Werewolf." The word had no sooner left Lexie's lips than Maddy instantly materialized to stand between them.

"Where's the werewolf? Who's a werewolf?" Maddy's neck was snapping around so quickly, Hudson feared she might rotate it too far—even all the way around—and cause mass hysteria among the guests. He clicked his throat at her warningly.

"Now I know why Pete's parents and our parents have always been so down on our friendship." Lexie's fists clenched. "They better not keep us apart."

"Keep you apart? It's not like you're going to marry him." Hudson laughed.

At this, Lexie suddenly looked exceptionally poetic and dreamy. "Who knows? Maybe I will, one day."

"Not unless I slay him first," declared Maddy.

"You better not!" hissed Lexie.

"I might!" Maddy cackled.

"Over my undead body!"

"Calm down, girls," warned Hudson. He wondered if all sisters fought like his. "We're in public, and one of the Argos is here. Trust me on this one—but if you want proof, go take another look at Dylan's cast, and the scuff marks by the pantry door."

He moved away before either of his baffled sisters could respond.

"Thanks for inviting me to your housewarming party," said Bethany Finn when her parents had come to collect her. "I'm changing my mind about you, Hudson. You always seemed stuck-up. But your family and where you live isn't exactly what I would have guessed. In a good way, I mean."

"I'm sorry if you thought I was stuck-up," said Hudson. Apologies weren't easy for him, but he hoped one day practice would make them a touch less rusty.

"Next year, I think you'll get a carnation," said Bethany. "You just might deserve it." She wriggled her eyebrows. An odd minx, that Bethany Finn.

As guests took leave, the old man had vanished. But Hudson could sense that he wasn't far away. After he helped his sisters and parents wash the dishes and put their house back to order, Hudson followed his hunch and ventured out onto the roof.

The city lights were up. Stars were scattered through the fog.

Mr. Schnur, in Orville form, was perched under the eaves. So still, he might have been a husk. Hudson summoned the energy to transform. It was getting easier for him. Just last week, he had transformed in broad daylight to help rescue Maddy. Now that he was gaining power, he knew that bigger Protections were in store for him. He just didn't know what they were. Yet.

He swung to hang upside down under the eaves so that

his face was level with Orville's. Up close, he could see the echo of Schnur. Strange.

"Stop switching off the heat generator at school," snapped the old hybrid. "It wastes power when you have to start it all up again."

"Sorry," apologized Hudson.

"Friendship is as important as clout," said Orville, more kindly.

"Yes," Hudson agreed.

"Your friends will be more helpful, going forward."

"I hope so."

"You will need them. There's still a lot to do," said Orville. "The earth isn't getting healthier. The humans aren't getting smarter. And the New World isn't getting any safer."

They sat together in silence for many hours. The temperature dropped. The wind changed. House lights went out. Hudson's eyes drooped. He folded his wings tight around his body and slept.

He woke at 4:00 to feel the familiar itch down his spine and through his shoulders. Swinging up from the drainpipe, he stretched, then moved to the edge of the building. His wings opened as easy as an umbrella between the flexible struts of his arms.

Orville was ready on his side. "Let's go."

Hudson looked down on the city. He bowed his head and plunged.

Madison Livingstone's
KILLER WHITE CHOCOLATE
MACADAMIA NUT COOKIES

Ingredients:

¹/₂ cup unsalted butter, softened

¹/₃ cup sugar

¹/₃ cup brown sugar, firmly packed

1 egg

1 tsp. vanilla

1 cup all-purpose flour

¹/₂ tsp. baking soda

¹/₄ tsp. salt

6¹/₂ oz. white chocolate, chopped

³/₄ cup macadamia nuts, halved

Directions:

Blend butter, sugars, egg, and vanilla until fluffy, stopping once to scrape down sides of bowl. Add flour, baking soda, and salt. Mix until lightly combined. Do not overmix. Stir in white chocolate chunks and nuts. Mound dough by ¹/₃ cupfuls onto lightly greased cookie sheet, spacing about 2 inches apart. Bake in preheated 350-degree oven until lightly brown around edges, about 12 minutes. Cool on cookie sheet for a few minutes, then remove to racks and cool completely. Store in an airtight container.

Watch closely when baking, as cookies will burn easily. If planning to slay vampires, replace nuts with two cups of softened, peeled, chopped garlic, and sub ¹/₂ cup of holy water for egg.

Lexington Livingstone's
BEST DOOMED QUOTES OF DOOMED POETS

Kurt Cobain (1967–1994) *"All alone is all we are."*

Hart Crane (1899–1932) *"My hands have not touched pleasure since your hands,— / No,—nor my lips freed laughter since 'farewell.'"*

Emily Dickinson (1830–1886) *"Heart, we will forget him, You and I, tonight! / You must forget the warmth he gave, I will forget the light."*

Sergei Esenin (1895–1925) *"In this life, dying is nothing new, / But living, of course, isn't novel either."*

Vachel Lindsay (1879–1931) *"Life's a jail where men have common lot. / Gaunt the one who has, and who has not."*

Jim Morrison (1943–1971) *"The future's uncertain and the end is always near."*

Sylvia Plath (1932–1963) *"The frost makes a flower, the dew makes a star, the dead bell, the dead bell.—Somebody's done for."*

Edgar Allan Poe (1809–1849) *"The Spirits of the dead, who stood In life before thee, are again In death around thee."*

Tupac Amaru Shakur (1971–1996) *"The world moves fast and it would rather pass by, / Than to stop and see what makes one cry."*

Percy Bysshe Shelley (1792–1827) *"Smiling they live, and call life pleasure / To me that cup has been dealt in another measure."*

Sara Teasdale (1884–1933) *"No one worth possessing / Can be quite possessed."*

My Life, So Far
By Hudson Livingstone
(before he tore it up into a hundred little pieces)

In the year of 1618, outside the rural province of
Pembrokeshire, I was received with great relief and
celebration as a firstborn son. Home was a cottage built
of wattle-and-daub. Father rented cattle and tilled fields
of barley. Mother kept goats and tended beehives. Our
Bess was a short-jointed mare, fourteen hands high.

Whilst I was yet in milk teeth, an early frost
blighted our harvest, followed by a winter so vengeful
and bitter we ate naught but winter root and stewed
fruit bat. Our misfortune was followed by a deadly
scourge of smallpox that devastated our populace. Being
of well-reputed herbal and medicinal skills, Mother
brewed a preserve of new milk and garlic clove against
infection. We prayed, fasted, and drank the conserve
thrice daily, to no avail. On first dread sight of skin
pustules, Father felled a sycamore and set to the task of
fashioning five long-nail coffins in preparation for a
decent family burial.

On the night we knew 'twould be our last on earth, we

stoked the hearth and huddled together for comfort. By chance, either our greatest fortune or darkest calamity, a shape-shifting vagrant came upon our wretched home. With intention to slake his terrible thirst, the beast punctured each of our necks with his most vengeful mark. By next sunrise, we were drained, weak— yet unrelieved by death. Whither the vat brew or stewed bat had been our talisman, we did not know. We persevered, and 'twas not long afore we were befriended by a secret colony of fellow hybrids and came to be enfolded into a larger family, safeguarded and disciplined by ancient Argos.

By day, we took to our coffin beds. By moonlight we scavenged the land for prey, siphoning small meals off healthy animals. A band of fruit hybrids, voicing dissention at this most unholy eternal life, took refuge in a ship bound for the New World. At that time, fear of the unknown barred our joining them. In the ensuing centuries, we resigned to grim existence until the end of the earth. Yet continued good news of the prosperous New World, and its possible blessing of mortality, drove our decision to emigrate. With permission and under the Argos' observance, we set forth for the New World's largest metropolis, New York City, where to our joy we believe that we have at long last escaped the curse of stopped time. We shall see.

It has been whispered that creatures of similar dark ilk, seeking refuge and solace, might live amongst us here. But I cannot speak of the verity of this rumor, and at this time must dismiss it as such.